Sweet

To Janet,
Thank you so much for your support. I hope you enjoy my first novel
Thank you.
Tylise Campbell

A Novel By Tylise Campbell

ISBN 0-9776428-0-1

AUTHOR INFORMATION
Tylise Campbell
Tycampbell23@yahoo.com

GRAPHIC DESIGNER INFORMATION
Cover image credits: Erin Ellis of EJDesigns
Ejdesigns4u@yahoo.com
www.ejdesigns4u.com

Printed in the U.S.A. by
Morris Publishing
3212 East Highway 30
Kearney, NE 68847
1-800-650-7888
Published by Tylise Campbell
For Next Up Publishing

Acknowledgments

First and above all else I would like to thank God, for being with me throughout my journey. Without you I am just flesh with no soul. Second I would like to thank my Mother for having faith in me and for supporting me throughout my 23 years. You are an angel from up above Mudder, and I wouldn't be here without you. I wuv you! I would also like to thank the rest of my family, my sister Ashika, for being you. Evil Ass! I love you sis. Joslyin for being the best little cousin in the world. I love you pretty girl. Shawn and that Man, I love yall. Gamma and Gammpa I love yall too! To my brother Lamar, I love you hairy nig. Lamar Jr and Lamya, Auntie Tylise loves yall very much. To my Daddy, I love you brutha and thinks for passing the crazy down to me! Just kidding. And the rest of my family thank you for being there, I love all of yall. Last but not least I want to thank my cuz, Erin aka Iron. I love you cuz, and I thank God you are in my life. It's our time, I can feel it. See you at the top! It's doo doo baby! LOL! Also I would like to thank You for supporting my first novel. I really appreciate it, and just remember this is just the beginning I'm not done yet. I'm like cake mix, watch me rise.

Be Blessed! Tylise Campbell

~A Sweet Start~

Andrea

"I do love you Raheem, but I don't think I'm in love with you."

I said trying to explain my confused feelings and emotions for this man, or young man. Silence fell over the conversation. I hated when Raheem got so quiet, as if my words and feelings meant nothing to him. He sat in silence like what I had just said was meaningless to him. He needs to learn how to express his feelings. He needs to grow up.

"Hello!" I yelled.

It seems Raheem only responded when I raised my voice at him. Just like a mother would yell at her child, just like an owner would yell at their animal, I would yell at Raheem.

"Yeah man, I'm here." He said nonchalantly.

"So what do you think about what I had to say?"

"Honestly?"

I hated when he said that, like I wanted to hear a lie. I think he just says stupid shit like that to fill the silence until he can think of something remotely intelligent to say in response.

"Yes Raheem, honestly."

"I think that is a bunch of bullshit. After all these years you all of a sudden find out that your not in love with me? That just doesn't sound logical Andrea. What are you hiding, why are you running away from our love? For you to sit here and tell me over the phone that you are no longer, or never were in love with me is bullshit. You know it and I know it, so what is really going on Andrea?"

Damn he knows me better than I thought he did.

"So your calling my feelings bullshit?" I said trying to make him look like the asshole he was making me out to be.

"Andrea, take it how you want. I love you and I will always love you, but you have to stop playing these damn games. I'm getting sick and tired of every time you find or even see someone else, you come up with a reason to break up with me. I'm sick of being on and off with you girl."

He was right about that. No matter how much I try to dress it up, I know I'm not right. Raheem knows me. After all these years he should. I wish I could say the same about him. He's so closed up. I only know what I beg to know from him, he never just opens up and lets me know anything without me having to ask. We have broke up to make up too many times. He is a good man though, but he's just not doing anything with his life right now. No job, not in school and living with his mom. Now what kind of future would I have with someone like that?

"You need time to work on yourself right now, you have a lot of shit you need to get straight." I said trying to be indirect about his situation.

"Do you think leaving me is going to help me get whatever issues you think I have straight?"

I couldn't hold back anymore, I tried to be nice but I guess he just doesn't get it.

"Raheem, you need to get the hell out of your momma's house, hop on the bus and find a job. Do something besides worry about me, and our relationship. You have so much going on in your life that needs your energy right now, and I'm not something that should be your main focus right now."

There I said it.

"That's how you feel Andrea? Fuck it then!"

Click.

No this fool did not just hang up on me. That is the kind of young and dumb shit I'm talking about. For him to be two years older than me, he acted like he was two years younger. I feel like I'm his mother sometimes. Maybe now he will grow up. I'm not tripping too much on us breaking up, cause it happens on the regular. It's like a routine with us. I break up with him, we don't talk for about a month or maybe longer, then he calls me and we get back together. I know that Raheem is going to be the man that I marry someday.

We need each other, mostly he needs me. I'm not going to tell him that though. Maybe he is right. I do play too many games. But he doesn't need to know that I feel that he is the man I am going to marry, then he really wouldn't do anything with his life. I'm like the incentive of his life. It's like if I do this then I'll get Andrea. And I know for a fact that he is not going to get with someone else. Don't get me wrong, he is not an ugly man. Not at all, in fact he is the total opposite of ugly. Brotha is fine, but Brotha got issues.

When I first met Raheem he had a fan club, literally. He was captain of the basketball team. Tall light and handsome. Raheem is about 6'4 and has a muscular build to him. He has these puppy dog type eyes, big and brown. And his lips, oh my God his lips, they are the juiciest, softest, plumpest, sexiest lips I have ever seen, kissed, licked or felt. Like satin pillows. Raheem has a hood look to him. He wears the baggy jeans, now not the type of jeans that hang off a brothas ass, that's just nasty, but the baggy fitting type of jeans. Being that its mostly pretty cold in Minnesota, he usually wears some type of name brand sweatshirt or sweater. Yeah he is rather sexy now that I think about it. I usually don't fall for the light skin brotha, and at first I didn't. He got on my nerves actually. I hated hearing his name in every females mouth, talking about how much they loved him. And in every guys mouth saying how much they wanted to be like him.

We got together by accident. My cousin invited me over to help her study, and when I walked in the door I saw him. I just knew he would be the typical dumb jock. But to my surprise we had a good time together. That's when I found out that he just wasn't this dumb jock, he actually had some kind of a brain in his head, but I guess that went away with time. I remember him walking me to the door and asking me for my phone number. I gave it to him, and in exchange he gave me a hug. I was so damn excited, I had never really had a relationship and it seemed that a relationship was approaching. When I went home I told my mother, bad idea. Her first question was of course who was his mother. I swear all mothers know each other from back in the day. And it wasn't a surprise when my mother knew his. She cautioned me about getting involved with someone so much older than me. I guess since at the time I was a sophomore and he was a senior, she thought I was going to be stupid. And I was. We ended up a couple after he graduated, and I thought I hit the jackpot.

This was my first real boyfriend, and I didn't know how to act. We didn't go out much, in fact we didn't go out at all. I always had an excuse on why I could not go out. Raheem would come over and watch movies but that was about it. Sounds fun right? I was envied by all the girls and wanted by all the guys. That's when all the trouble started. Girls would call and leave sexy messages on his phone, and the guys would tell Raheem they each had a piece of me. That really got to him because he hadn't had sex with me. He would accuse me of everything under the sun after his so-called "boys" would tell him the things I had supposedly done.

The sex thing was a big issue at first. I think because he had been so used to getting sex whenever he wanted it. Its not like I was holding out because I wanted to play games, honestly I was just scared. Raheem didn't believe that though. He once had the balls to ask me if he could have sex with his friend, Jazmin. Bold motherfucker. He tried to tell me that it wouldn't mean anything because they were both in relationships. Basically he told me to give it up or to let him get it from somewhere else. When I told him, "Hell no!", he told me he couldn't be with me any more and hung up the phone. I cried my eyes out all night while listening to "Love Hurts" by Jon B. and watching Apollo reruns. The next day I went to his house with my puffy eyes and begged for him to come back to me. My fat eyes must have done the trick, cause I have had him since that day. And I haven't given up anything yet, and I do not plan on it anytime soon. At least not until he gets his shit together. I don't know if he has had sex with someone while we were together, but I doubt it. He loves me too much. Right now Raheem is probably leaving me a message begging for me to come back to him.

"You have no new messages." My answering

machine announced.

Well there should be a message sooner or later. In the mean time in between time I got to get on with my love life. I can't just sit around and wait for him to get it together. He better not even think about trying to get another chick, even if he does she won't be better than I am, that's for damn sure. I'll call once every two weeks just to check up on him, to let him know I'm waiting on him to get straight. The truth is I'm not waiting for shit, but he doesn't need to know that.

"May I speak with Andrea please?", a deep sexy voice asked.

"This is she, who is calling?"

"Javonte, I met you about three weeks ago, So how have you been?"

Now Javonte is the chocolate brotha I need in my life right now. He is not universally fine like Raheem is. He is one of those acquired taste type of brothas. I don't feel bad about going down the ladder instead of up. It's like the less attractive the guy is, the more he will appreciate a woman like me. Yeah Javonte is going to be the one I'm with during my lunch break from Raheem. I don't plan on falling for this guy. He is just something to do right now.

"I've been fine."

"I didn't ask you how you looked, I asked how you were doing." Javonte said trying to be funny. I wanted to tell him to try harder, but I went along with it.

"Oh, I get it. I've been good, so what have you been up too?"

"Nothing much, I just got out of a relationship, so I've just been laying back, ya know?"

Damn this brotha got straight to the point.

"That's too bad, how long ago did you two break up?" I asked getting ready to do the math.

"About a week and a half ago, I couldn't take her shit any more."

"Almost two weeks ago huh? And how many weeks ago did you ask for my number?" I asked trying to catch him up in a lie.

"Yeah I was wrong for approaching you while I was still in a relationship, but it was just something about your sexy dark brown skin that drew me to you."

I guess since Javonte his self is dark skinned, he didn't use the usual line, which is a good thing. Usually I hear this line from 90% of the men that approach me, "Damn you sure are fine to be a dark skinned sista." Whatever the hell that means. Do these men think that is some kind of compliment? Like being dark skinned is some kind of disability that I overcame. I mean being a good looking dark sista shouldn't be some kind of miracle. I guess I should just take the compliment and be happy that I am blessed. Like they say, the darker the berry, the sweeter the juice. I have dark brown skin that is smooth and flawless. I have light brown eyes, but they actually change from light in the winter and dark in the summer. It's that Indian in me from my Grandfather I guess.

I just wish that Indian would have kicked in when it came to my hair, I guess that's the straight up African in me. I keep it permed but most if not all of the time you can't see my hair. Yes I am a recipient of packaged hair. I usually change my hair style every two weeks, but right now its long, straight and black. It's quite sexy. My lips are cute to me, but let my friends tell it, I have lips like a white person. Which sounds stupid to me, because I have seen plenty of white people with lips bigger than mine. As long as I like my lips I'm just fine. They go with my face though, so it's all good. I'm like 5'5 when I'm not wearing heals. The first thing that men usually notice about me are my eyes. Yeah right! The first thing that they notice is my freaking 36 double d's. I'm not chunky so they are very noticeable. Have you ever noticed that most of the time when you have one, meaning breasts, you usually don't have the other, meaning a big ass and vice versa. Well unless you live down south, cause I have seen some country chicks with banging bodies. It must be something in the water. I wish they would bottle that shit up and ship it up here. Anyways back to my ass, I didn't have a big ass at first, but as time went on, it just came. Its not as big and fat as I want it to be, but hey I work with what I got.

"That is the reason why I took my time calling you, I wanted to respect you and my relationship at the same time. But I know that still doesn't excuse my actions." Javonte finished.

Alright, this is too good to be true. This is a man that admitted when he was wrong, and showed respect for me and his relationship. I bet he could make a cold blooded murder sound acceptable.

"I understand. I just got out of a relationship myself."

"So I guess we could say I was wrong for asking for the number, and you were wrong for giving it out right?"

"Since when is giving your number to a potential friend considered to be wrong?" I said. Javonte laughed.

"Yeah okay Andrea, if you say so." We both laughed.

"So how long were you and your guy together?" He asked.

"A long time, a little more than five years. How about you and your chick?"

"You got me beat, that's for sure. We were

together for about six months, and that was on and off, so probably shorter than that."

"What was the problem." I asked getting the details, so I could do the total opposite.

"She was crazy, flat out crazy. I would wake up and see her right in my face, and I don't have any idea how she got in my house. She would follow me everywhere, she tapped my phones, and the girl even put cameras all up in my house. I hope you're not crazy like that Andrea."

"Damn, yeah that is crazy. You don't have to worry about me. I'm nothing like that. I might break into your house a couple of times, but I would never tap your phone." I said jokingly.

He laughed, luckily. Most people don't get my sarcasm. He was a cool guy, not into the whole relationship thing right now. Just into the friends with benefits thing, and I had no problem with that. Sometimes a girl just wanted to be held, kissed and cuddled without all those lies that men give us. Javonte seems too good to be true, but I'll go along with it. I wonder what Raheem is doing. I wonder why he hasn't called yet?

"So what was the deal with you and your ex? That is a long time to be in a relationship with someone, it must have been hard to just give all those years up?"

"Well yeah, but it's not like we won't still keep

in contact."

"Oh I see, your just gonna keep him around for the booty calls and go on about your business right?"

No this man didn't. How dare he assume that I would be that shallow to where as I couldn't have a platonic relationship with an ex boyfriend, or a male for that matter. See I knew it was too good to be true. My mother always told me, "If it sounds too good to be true, then Andrea, it probably is." I know now. I get my hopes up too quickly, it's like I give them too much slack and that's the reason why when someone lets me down, it hurts more then it should.

"Actually Javonte, it's not like that at all. Can I ask you a question? What have I done or said that gave you the impression that I was that type of female. I mean for you to say something so judgmental and direct about someone that is unknown to you is very bold, especially when you really haven't even taken the time to get to know anything about that person?"

Lets see if he could talk his way out of this one.

"You really haven't done anything to make me think that you are that type of person, that's why I asked. I don't know many ex boyfriends that are still friends with their ex girlfriends. The whole idea sounds rather oxy moronic don't you think? I mean if you can't be in a relationship with that person, what makes you think you can have a friendship with that same person?"

"No one is ever the same person as they are when they are in a relationship Javonte. You won't treat your homeboys the same way you treat your girl friend would you? And I'm sure you wouldn't curse and talk to your mother the same way you talk to your friends. Right? People treat different relationships differently, so if I'm in a relationship with you then things are one way and if we are just plain friends, then things are another way."

Now what could he possibly say now.

"I see what you mean, but shouldn't the person you're in a relationship with be one of your closest friends anyway?"

"Yes they should." I hesitated to say, I could see exactly where he was going with this.

"Well then shouldn't you treat them the same way and expect the same things. I mean a friend is a friend no matter what prefix or suffix you add to the word. And if indeed you and your ex where friends and the relationship didn't work out, what makes you this that taking the boy off of the friend will make him a different person."

Damn it! See I don't like it when someone enlightens me on a topic that I thought I knew so much about. I'm supposed to be the deep one in the conversation, I'm supposed to be the one who enlightens not gets enlightened.

"Yeah I get what your saying, I guess." I

understood exactly what he was saying, but the situation between Raheem and I is very different. So Javonte's outlook on the whole friends after a relationship thing doesn't apply to Raheem and me. It just isn't our situation.

"Sorry if I offended you by assuming you where the booty call type, I guess that was my indirect way of asking, or of seeing exactly what type of woman you were."

"Yeah okay, next time just ask. It's much easier that way."

"Sounds too easy, sometimes the best way is the hard way. Besides I got to see how you felt about the whole men and women being friends. The hard way just provoked a deeper conversation, but I feel you on the whole idea of just coming out and asking. Sometimes I can find a better answer in a discussion rather than in an answer to a single question."

There is nothing wrong with a deep guy in fact, I encourage it, but not in the first minutes of a conversation. Shit! Shut the hell up and tell me how pretty I am, and how much you want to take me out and wine and dine me. Then after all the flattery we can get intellectual.

"Yeah I got you. So you graduate this year right?"

I had to change the subject for now, and get all the simple getting to know you questions out of the way.

"Thankfully I'm finally graduating. This is my fifth year at the University."

"So what is your major?"

"Well my major is sports medicine, but that's not really my first career choice. Hopefully I make it big and get drafted in the NFL."

"You play football for the University?"

I never heard of a Javonte on the team, he must ride the bench, and just have those pipe dreams of making off the bench and scoring five touchdowns in a row and getting drafted that same week.

"I'm Javonte Chamberlain."

Okay, thanks for the last name, but I still don't know who the hell you are. I should have said that but I'm too nice.

"Javonte Chamberlain huh." I said pretending I knew who he was.

"J.C., the starting quarterback for the Gophers. You don't come to many games do you?"

Oh my goodness J.C. I'm so stupid. Damn. This brotha was good. I'm at all the games cheering on this faceless man in armor topped with a jersey. I heard he had plenty of teams offer him deals. Oh shit, not another jock. I can't have two in a row. I'll just be setting my self up to get let down. I guess it's just a friend thing anyway, but still.

"Yeah I'm a big fan. I just wasn't thinking right. It's good to finally put a face to that overused name. No offense."

"None taken."

"So playing for the NFL is like a major dream of yours right?"

"Yeah I've been playing ever since I can remember. But I'm realistic, I do know that there is a chance that I won't make it into the League, that's why I'm majoring in sports medicine. That way if I don't make it to the top, I can at least work close to the game."

"That's smart, but I'm sure you'll make it into the NFL. I heard you could have gone into the draft your second year."

"Yeah but I wanted to finish school first, but between me and you I did get an unofficial offer from the Vikings last month."

Between me and you my ass. Everybody and thier momma knew that shit. Oh wait a minute, maybe I should try to get with Javonte. He's talking about making to the big time, and I'm sure he'll need his little trophy wife to be in the stands and at parties right by his side. He sounds like a guarantee to the good life.

"That's good, good luck with everything." I said trying to sound not as interested in the subject of football, even though I watched every game and knew every term in the book.

"So what's your major?" He asked.

"Film." I said. Short and sweet, no double major, no minor just film. Simple as that.

"Oh so you want to do the whole movie thing huh, like what types of movies. Big time, pornos, independent what?"

Men always have to bring up sex some how, why is that. Well I guess I would always think about it if my sex tool was outside my body and in my face every day, but my hands are in my face every day and I don't talk or think about them all the time. Take your time with that one. I'm a virgin and like Talib Kweli says, I got to do what I got to do, just to get by.

"Hopefully big budget type movies, but whatever happens."

"That sounds interesting, had you ever watched a porno with your ex?"

What the hell type of question? And where in the world did it come from. I'll never fully understand men. I see where his mind is. Typical.

"No, I'm sorry to say I haven't."

"I guess with you two together for so long you never had to do anything like that, all you had to do was do the damn thing, no point for the porno help huh?"

What! Well I guess its about time to throw in my shocker, lets see how long it takes for this one to run.

"Well this might sound surprising, but I'm not sexually active."

"Wow, I don't know many twenty something, or any females eighteen and up for that matter that are still virgins."

"Is that a good thing?"

"It's an um. It's a surprising thing."

He didn't answer my question. They never do at this point of the conversation.

"So is that a good or bad thing that Im a virgin?"

"It's a good thing, it's a commendable thing, I commend you for your choice, it's a good commendable thing, I mean choice, it's a good commendable choice."

Whatever. I bet he can't wait to see if he can take it from me. At this point that's probably his main goal now. His main focus is going to be trying to say the right things, to make me lower my guard and eventually my pants. Yeah I bet it's a good thing.

"I'm glad you feel that way, I take it you have dipped and dabbed in the whole intercourse act. No pun intended."

"Yeah I have, I don't know many men that haven't. It's not all that it is cracked up to be though. I think that sex is maybe 10% of a relationship and the other 90% is all about the mental connection rather than the physical."

Negro please! Sounds good. I see that operation devirgination has begun.

Step One: Make the potential victim believe that you honestly think that sex is not important.

Step Two: Show her you really do care about her thoughts and feelings.

Step Three: Do not under any circumstance make any sexual references in her presence.

I'm not new to this game. I guess I should act like I believe his bullshit.

"I'm so glad you feel that way. I don't know many men that feel that way, you in fact are rare."

"Can you hold on one second that's my other line?"

"Sure."

Does he think I don't know that he just pushed the damn flash button to make it sound that way? Like I'm dumb, damn.

"Hello, I'm sorry about that, it's my coach, will it be all right if I called you back later on?"

"That would be fine, being that I don't have

your number you would have to call me back in order for us to speak again."

I had to let it be known that I had no way of calling him, so his excuse for not calling me wouldn't be, "I was waiting on you." The ball is in his court now.

"Okay then, Ima holla to you later."

Click

The whole virgin thing always scares them off. I'm used to it though, it's a fat chance that I'll hear from Javonte again. Although that would be a complete loss for my guaranteed future. I have always dreamed of just being taken care of by my man. Oh well. I guess I should check my messages.

"You have one new message," my answering machine announced.

It must be Raheem, being that I was on the phone and I do have call waiting I would have heard it if he had called. Raheem always records his message from his phone, then sends it to me. Why he just doesn't call me, I'll never know. I guess it occupies his time. I wonder what he has to say. This should be good.

Elongai

I was awakened from my comfortable slumber by the smell of breakfast being cooked in my designer kitchen. As I wiped the sleep from my eyes, I realized that there shouldn't be anyone in my house. What the hell was going on? While running down my long hallway toward my kitchen, I stumbled over articles of clothing. It seems as if my intruder had made themselves very comfortable. When I finally reached the kitchen, I saw him, this naked man in my mother fucking kitchen, cooking my mother fucking food!

"Who the hell are you, and what the hell are you doing in my kitchen?", I yelled.

"You know who I am, and you know why I'm here Elongai," The mystery man calmly said.

No the fuck I didn't know who this was, and why they were here in my damn kitchen.

"I advise you to get out before I call the police, after I beat your ass, now get the fuck out!", I said while grabbing a knife.

Then all of a sudden, this man walked over toward me, this naked man, who I had never seen in my life was walking toward me and I couldn't move. I was stuck, I was excited, I was confused. The mystery man walked right past me, then turned around and whispered to me.

"Come with me Elongai, Come join me Elongai."

I was hypnotized. I followed this man into my bedroom while removing my clothes. I followed this man, this perfect stranger into my designer bedroom. He laid down on my bed, his manhood was as stiff as the black power fist, and so was mine. I couldn't help but to join him on my bed, both of our buff bodies pulsating with lust. Then it happened this man kissed me.

"Good Morning Minneapolis, if you're supposed to be at work at 7:00 then you got fifteen minutes, so wake up, wake up, wake up!", the radio alarm clock roared.

"Oh, thank God that was just a dream.", I said to myself in relief.

"What was just a dream honey?", My wife asked.

"Um, you know that one dream we all have where we are falling off a building, and we wake up right before we hit the ground and die?", I said with my head in my pillow. "Well that was the dream I just had baby."

I hated lying to my wife, but not when her feelings were at risk. I just made sure I didn't look her in the eyes when I did lie to her. Her sexy innocence would have disabled my lying capabilities completely.

My wife is so damn fine. Tamia, that's her name,

is what most would call the video girl type, or model type. She is 5'9, luckily I'm 6'6 so her height doesn't really bother me much. She has a butter pecan skin color, a step under having light skin. She has these bright eyes, which can easily convert from innocent to sexy in a split second. Tamia's hair is fluffy, she calls it naturally curly, I call it fluffy. It looks like golden cotton candy. Its like gold, tan, light brown, I don't know, it looks tan to me but she says its light brown, so its light brown. She wears these hazel contacts to match her hair, it works for me, she's sexy either way. One thing that is so sexy about my wife is her tattoo in the middle of her lower back, and guess what it says. "*Elongai,*" that's right, my name! That shit is so sexy to me. I haven't gotten her name yet, but I have a phobia of needles so she understands. Another sexy thing she has is this belly button ring that lights up in the dark, it's not in now, but when it is, damn I can't even explain it. Oh and her lips, I have never in my life seen lips this sexy, this perfect. It's like when I kiss my wife, every thought is replaced with her, it's like the first time every time. The same thing with sex with us. That might sound bad to some, and good to some, but let me explain my feelings on the whole sex thing. It's like I never know what to expect when it comes to the bedroom part of our relationship.

One day it might be soft, slow and sweet with the candles, soft music and all. But the next night, its props like swings and whips, and the sex isn't slow its fast, and not soft its rough, and no candles and soft music in the background, its red and blue light bulbs in the lamps, and Uncle Luke playing. I love it. I love her.

"So you going to work today El baby?"

"Only if the bills need to be paid, if not I think I just might stay in bed with you Mia." I said as I gave my wife her morning hug.

"Shut up boy, don't act like I want to be in this bed all day and not out working, just remember you're the one that knocked me up!" Tamia said as she smacked my arm from around her.

Tamia is eight months pregnant with our first child, it's a boy, or that's what the doctors say. She had the room painted blue, so it better be a boy, or a girl that likes blue.

"I love you Mia." I always said that to end a conversation, even if it's not a bad one, I just say it to change the subject.

"What time you got to be at the office El?"

"My first appointment isn't until about eleven or twelve in the afternoon, so I have time to spend with you and your stomach."

I work as a photographer for a magazine that I just so happen to own called *Juicy*. Such a sexy name. Tamia is lucky that she has a man like me in her life, she really didn't even have to work if she didn't want to. But let her tell it, she is "an independent woman," and she does not need any man for anything. I'll believe it when I see it. Tamia is the envy of most women, to have a man like me, fine *and* employed, she should be. Now don't get me wrong I'm not conceded, but I do know how I look, and I'm proud of that. I'm so fine that I used to be a model, not by choice though, but I needed to do something to support my wife at 20 years old. Like I said, I'm tall, 6'6. I'm brown, not dark, not light, just brown. I used to be clean shaven when I modeled but now I have a low goatee. I wear my hair in a fade, with waves that would make you sea sick! I have dark brown slanted eyes. They are what helped me get those modeling jobs. I have structured lips, not boxy, just structured. They have reason, they build my facial features, they give my face the chiseled effect. That's what I was told. I'm a buff guy, I work out a lot so it's not like the chubby kind of buff, but the muscle kind of buff. Not as big as a body guard, but not smaller than the model Tyson. Actually now that I think about it, I have almost the same type of build, only a little bigger. And I wear a size 13 ½ shoe, need I say more.

"Do you mind making me and my stomach some scrambled eggs and heat up some of those spare ribs from last night, oh and can you bring me some bread and a jar of mayo too please?"

"Before or after my shower?" I asked hoping she wouldn't say what I thought she was going to say.

"Before our shower if you don't mind, I'm really hungry."

Yeah, she said what I dreaded to hear. "Our shower." We had a two person shower not a three person shower, but I would have to be a fool to tell her that. Don't get me wrong, pregnant women are a beauty and Tamia is still as sexy as she was when we married almost five years ago, but that damn belly gets in the way. I just have to keep telling myself that my son will be out of there in a couple of weeks and our showers will be the same once again.

"No problem honey, I'll bring that up for you in a couple of minutes."

Tamia and I got married fast and at a young age. We met when we were 18 years old and we got married when we were 20. Fast don't you think. But we were in love back then, and we still are. The due date of our son is ironically the same day as our fifth year anniversary. That would sure be something special if it happens like that, but most likely it won't. It was rough at first, being so young, but we made it. I own my own company and Tamia works for me as the editor.

"Elongai can you bring me a strawberry soda too please?", my wife yelled from up stairs. I liked it better when she called me El, Elongai sounds so funny. It's pronounced E-long-gay. It sounds like a porn star's name to me.

"Mia, I don't see any strawberry soda in here." I yelled up.

"I know it's at the corner store, can you run and get me some please?"

This was my chance to get out of "our shower." With my fingers crossed I yelled back.

"Tamia I'm not going to the store looking like this, let me hop in the shower first, then I'll go get your strawberry soda while your food stays warm in the oven, okay?"

"Okay. Whatever just hurry up El!"

She was mad, but oh well she'll forget about it when she gets her breakfast served to her in bed. I'm kind of glad that she asked, or ordered me to go to the store for her. That way I could have sometime to think about those crazy ass dreams I have been having. What do they mean? And why in the world am I having them on a regular basis? I know I'm not gay, how could I be? I'm married to one of the finest women on this earth, I'm about to have my first child and I'm happy. Not happy meaning gay, but emotionally happy. I have had this dream almost once a month for the past year. I haven't told anyone about these dreams yet, and I don't know if I ever will. I can just guess how my friends would intrepid these dreams.

"How are you today sir?", the bag boy at the corner grocery store asked me.

"I'm doing just fine, and yourself?", I asked just to be polite.

"Could be better, but hey that's life!"

I chuckled, and looked up to match this cheerful voice with a face. Oh shit! This was the man in my dreams.

"Hope it gets better," I said in a hurry and got the fuck out of dodge.

I can't believe it, what was all of this telling me. Oh I got it, its one of those connecting dreams. I started having these dreams right before my wife got pregnant, it was a sign that I would be spending a lot of my time in the grocery store in the future. And the reason why I got in the bed with this naked man was because the naked man represents the food that my wife consumes, being that he bags it up. This dream is just me telling myself that I can't wait until I am able to make love to my wife once again, without all that weight or "food," in the way! That's it, that's logical! Damn I'm glad I thought of that, I'm glad I looked up and seem that mans face. Everything happens for a reason. Maybe I should jog back home.

"Baby I got your strawberry soda, I'll be up in a minute," I yelled up stairs.

I'm so glad there was a logical explanation to my weird ass dreams.

"I hope your still hungry Mia?", I said as I tried

to balance myself on our black iron carousel stairs.

"What where you dreaming about last night Elongai, what where you really so relieved about?" Mia said with her arms crossed over her chest.

"What are you talking about girl? Just eat drink and be marry."

Damn why was she bringing this up? I just got this off my mind?

"Look at this Elongai, and you tell me what I'm talking about." Tamia said.

As she pulled back our grey down comforter, I saw what she was talking about. There it was a wet spot. A mother fucking wet spot on my sheets, on my side of the bed. A wet spot that was the product of a male, not a female, not the usual wet dream suspect, but a male! Oh shit, I thought I was just hot and sweaty, how could I not realize that was there. How could I not feel that shit and how will that fit into my logical equation?

"Baby I didn't know that was there."

"I didn't ask you if you knew it was there, I asked you what you were dreaming about to create it Elongai, now tell me the truth. I'll understand if you were having fantasies about having sex with a more attractive woman, just tell me the truth El." She insisted.

Anyway it goes, I'm up shit creek without a

paddle. If I tell her the truth, she will never look at me the same, and if I tell her what she already is thinking, then she will think I'm dreaming about other women. Or that I'm cheating on her and that I am no longer attracted to her. I know how my wife thinks.

"Okay Tamia the truth is, I have been having these dreams about you, without all the weight you have gained, in these dreams we make love how we used to. That's why I woke up and said I'm glad that was just a dream, because I can't imagine you without our son. Mia I love the way we make love right now. It makes me feel so bad when I dream about you without our child, and it makes me feel so bad baby. I'm so sorry that this happened like this. I love you the way you are okay?"

"I love you too El, it's alright I understand. Just don't feel bad about it. It's normal. I was reading about it in my ' Be Prepared', magazine. Come here and give me a hug."

"I'm so sorry, I feel so bad Mia," I said putting the icing on the cake. I hated lying but not when I could prevent from hurting her.

"So how about we take our shower after you finish your breakfast, so we can wash away our blues?" I owed it to her. It was the least I could do.

"I love you El." My overly understanding wife said.

"I love you too Mia. I love you too."

"And don't worry I won't make you take two showers, and I think I'd rather be alone anyway, so it looks like we both win." Tamia said as she carried her breakfast down stairs into the kitchen.

"I didn't mind taking two showers, but if you want to be alone, I understand."

"I bet you do." She said as she threw some food up the stairs at me and laughed.

Thankfully she wasn't upset about the whole thing. I'm glad she laughed. It made me feel a whole lot better about what was going on.

"I guess I should change the bedding, so which color do you want on the bed now?" I asked my wife just to be nice, even though she had no decorating sense. If only she decorated the way she dressed, our house would be lovely. But she left that up to me.

"Surprise me." She yelled up.

We yelled a lot, but not in a bad way. We have never had a huge major argument before, just little disagreements. Which is a good thing, I don't think I would know how to react if we ever had a big argument.

"Will do!" I yelled back.

Being that our master bedroom walls were white with bright teal trim, we had some pretty wild colors on our bed. This soaked grey one was one of the mild ones. Just to liven things up in the bedroom, I suppose I'll put the teal, blue and green print on the bed. That one makes our bed look like a clear water bed, with teal, blue and green water in the inside. It is one of the more tropical prints. And of course, when I changed the bed covers, I had to change the four lamps we had in our bedroom. We have multi color lamp shades to give our room more of a harmonious look to it. My wife thinks I go over board sometimes, but I have to feel comfortable about where I lay my precious head. Our whole house is coordinated, from top to bottom. The basement has stone walls, with black leather furniture. The pool table is black and so are the doors down there. The carpet is grey of course. The entertainment center, which holds the big screen and stereo system is also black. It's a nice feel down in the basement. The first level is all white, which must get changed since we are having a child. Maybe the first level will be converted to off white. The first level includes, a bathroom, kitchen, living room, den and my office is also down there. All of the walls are white, it has a heavenly effect.

The basement was white at first, but Tamia insisted on changing it to black, so now its black. It matches the piano so I'm fine with that. The second level is where our bedroom is. We also have two other rooms on the second level. One is blue, our sons room, with white trim. The other room is white with yellow trim. On the last level, the third floor is split into two parts. One is my wife's office, and the other is my photo studio. We live a pretty good life I suppose. We live right off of Lake Calhoun in South Minneapolis. The only thing that allows us to fit in here is our money. There are not many black folks around the lake area. We found a couple, but their skin color is about the only way I could tell that they were black. We're not that far from black folks though. All we have to do if we want to see some color, is go straight up Lake Street, deep into South Minneapolis, and there they are. North and South Minneapolis is where it's at. I have friends that live over in North Minneapolis, so I see my fair share of brown folks.

Minnesota isn't as bad as people think, there are black people here. Many, many black people. What I say is Minnesota is not as black as Atlanta and not as white as Europe, so we are somewhere in the middle. I like it here, I'm happy here. Emotionally happy I mean.

"Telephone baby." Mia yelled up to me.

"What up El?"

"What's going on brotha, how are things going with you?", I asked my friend. We have known each other ever since we both were wearing diapers, he's like the brother I never had.

"Nothing much, just going up and down again."

"You and Andrea broke up again?" I asked in scripted astonishment.

He and Andrea were always braking up and making up. They got that strong love like Mia and I got, but I don't think they are as mature as we are with it. That's why they go through all this teenage bullshit. I can't wait til he grows out of this, cause to tell you the truth, I'm sick of hearing about it, but that's what friends are for right.

"Yeah, again, I can't take this shit man. I can't take getting my heart broken every other week. I know I'm a man and all that, but to be real with you my heart can't take this shit anymore. You feel me?"

"Then don't. It's all on you Raheem."

Listening to this shit makes me grateful that I'm married.

"Yeah I know, but.."

"El, something is wrong, I think the baby is coming! El come down here! I think its time." My wife screamed.

"I gotta go man something is wrong with Mia. I'll call you back ASAP!" I hung up.

"Mia baby I'm coming, its gonna be alright!" I yelled as I ran and fell down the steps, damn spiral steps you can't run on those bad boys. Why was it time, she wasn't due for another one ½ months, is this normal?

"El hurry up, I think something is wrong." She cried as I ran back down stairs after running back up to get her purse and my cell phone.

She was lying in the hallway near the kitchen, I couldn't tell if she is alright or not.

"I'm right here baby. Mia get up. Mia?"

No answer.

"Mia, Mia baby, get up. Can you hear me? Mia!"

Andrea

"What up Andrea it's me Raheem, I was calling to apologize for hanging up on you. You just make me mad when you come out of the blue with your shit. I just want to let you know that I love you and I want to be with you, but I'm not going to beg you to love me the way I love you. Maybe we should just take sometime away from each other, just to see if what I need is not in you, and if what you need is not in me. You know what I'm trying to say. We just need to take sometime apart to look for what we really need. If we are meant to be then we will be. So I won't call you or write you and I want you to do the same. I think this will be good for us. I love you and hope we will be together soon."

Okay what just happened? Since when does he have the upper hand in this relationship. Where does he get the nerve to tell me not to call or write him? Are you serious? Is this for real? If he wants a little break from reality then that is what he will get. I know one thing though, he better not get mad at me when I find somebody better than him. Because I know for a fact, he won't find anyone that can hold a candle to me. I'll give him his little punk ass break. Maybe this is a sign. Maybe its time for me to move on and just start all over. That's so hard though. It's nice to know that even if it doesn't work out between me and one guy, then I always have Raheem. He's like my back up plan. I guess that sounds kind of mean, but at least I'm honest. Its times like this that I'm thankful to have a male friend to help me to understand what exactly goes on inside of a man's head.

"Hey Drea what up?"

"What's up Malik? Me and Raheem are having problems again. Well Raheem is the one having problems. They just got passed down to me."

Malik was my male friend that helps me understand this underdeveloped species that we call Man. Malik and I grew up together, but we kind of fell off during High School, but fell back together soon after that. He is why I don't understand why people say that it's impossible to be friends with a man, and not have sex, feelings or even urges to be together. Malik has never tried to hook up with me, and I have never tried to get with him.

I guess it helps that he's gay. But you would never know it by looking at Malik, but after you talk to him for a while it just slips right out. Now don't get me wrong, he's not one of these undercover brothas out here. You know the kind that are gay but don't look it, so they still feel they have the right to mess around with women and men and not tell either of them. Now that is just wrong. No he is not one of those, that's not his style. Now sometimes I get confused on his sexuality, sometimes he's as straight as my hair after a fresh perm. Just so he won't feel left out of the male bonding with his father. Then in the same breath he is strictly dickly. I guess all that matters is that he's happy with his choices in love. And being as cute as he is, I'm sure he will have plenty to choose from.

Malik has this pretty brown skin that reminds me of rich milk chocolate. His teeth are white and straight, breath always fresh, and his clothes are always pressed and clean. His eyes should have a caution sign that reads, *"Feelings of deepness may occur if looked into for long periods of time."* He's about 6'2, not skinny but not buff either. He used to be a print model. He's one of those guys that pose for things like male hair grease or even Sean Jean. But mostly he is modeling underwear in those Target ads. Right now he's just doing odd jobs here and there to make ends meet. Maybe he thinks he's going to get discovered walking down the snowy streets of North Minneapolis. I hope not.

"Girl when are you just going to move on, you're cute I'm sure you can find someone else."

Malik hated the fact that Raheem and I were still dealing with each other. He told me I needed to move on a week after I met Raheem, so how am I suppose to honestly know when to listen to Malik, and when not to.

"It's not about finding someone, its about finding someone I can connect with."

"Oh like the way you and Raheem connected.

After all these years of knowing him, you know the same about him as you did after a month of dating him."

He was right, but that's not the point. The point is we have some kind of bond that time has allowed us to have.

"We have a bond Malik."

"Whatever Andrea. I think you're just scared that you won't find anyone that will be on your tip the way his lame ass was. Following you around like a lost puppy dog. You want a toy not a man. You want a son not a man."

"Shut up Malik, I don't even know why I try to talk to your ass sometimes. I think the reason why you don't want me and Raheem to be together, is because you want to be with him. Now how do you like them apples baby boy." He hated when I said things like that, but I hated when he made a point that made me look bad.

"I think those apples a just bitter and mad, because I'm so juicy and sweet. And if I want Raheem's ass, trust me I could have it. I could have it on a stage, in a pink J. Lo one piece singing and stepping to any song by Jill Scott. Now I do like to travel but baby please do not take me there."

I swear his gayness comes and goes. When that bitch comes out its time for me to retreat, and change the subject.

"Alright Malik. I thought you had to work today?"

"I did but they let me off early which rained on my parade. I needed to make some extra cash this week, but if business is slow then I have no choice but to go."

"If you need some extra cash I could talk to my girl to see if she has some open slots coming up."

"Yeah hook it up. But for now I have get going, so I'll talk to you a little later, and don't forget to hook me up with that job, what kind of print is it anyways?"

"Oh just some naked pictures for those women only magazines."

"Girl how broke I am, I will be happy to show my ashy ass for some cash!"

"I hope it never gets that bad for you Malik, I was just kidding. I'm not sure what kind of things they are doing right now, but I'll find out and get back to you."

"Well okay, I'll talk to you later, Bye Sweetheart."

"Later Leaky."

El

"Just breathe baby, just breathe." I said to my wife trying not to sound as frantic as I felt.

For an instant I thought it was all over, I thought I had lost my wife. I thought I had lost my child. For an instant I thought I had lost my life.

"El please shut up and drive. This shit hurts." My wife screamed.

I drove like a bat out of hell, like the cops were chasing me and my name was Rodney King. I was flying.

"We are almost there baby please, just breathe, like the white lady taught you in class, hee hee hoo, hee hee hoo."

"Are you mocking me nigga? Let me pull down on your balls and you try to breathe." Mia said with fire in her eyes and power in her voice. That was my cue to shut the hell up.

"My wife she's going into labor, she's only eight months, please can someone get a doctor!"

They rushed over to the car, I was praying they didn't dent my Mercedes with the wheelchair. I know that should have been the last thing on my mind but damn.

"Sir you might want to call your families, and let them know the baby is its way." The doctor informed me.

I am not ready for this, not right now, not this fast. I had at least one more month to get myself together, to get my mind right and all that jazz. Besides I didn't even finish reading the parenting book Tamia bought me. I don't know how to change no diapers, or rock babies to sleep. Shit I'm a man I'm heavy handed I might mess something up.

"Hey it's me El, Mia is in labor, the baby should be here soon." I said sounding like a broken record.

I called about fifty people, and I'm not even half way done. Luckily I was getting mostly answering machines. It seemed like when I got a live person, they wanted to ask fifty thousand questions. Like they were the only phone call I had to make. I was beginning to lose my patience.

"You ready for this pretty boy!" I heard a voice shout from outside the door. When the face emerged, I wasn't surprised. It was Mia's father. He hated me.

"Harold please." Mia's mother said, sounding just as delicate as a baby bird, but looked at me like a hungry vulture.

"I just can't wait to see what that cocky bastard is gonna do when he has to pay attention to someone other than himself." Mr. Jones said. He just had to finish his worthless thought.

"Daddy please this is not the time nor place, sit

down." Mia said while bending over to get her epidural.

"Okay Mrs. Blaque, please be very still." The doctor said trying to clam my wife down.

"How you doing Mr. and Mrs. Jones?" I asked trying to be polite, but I could careless about how they were doing. I knew they could not stand me. Tamia's parents were some uppity black folks. You know the kind. They get an extra zero in their bank account and they think they're better than the rest of us.

"We are fine son, but it's not us you should be worried about." Mia's mother said. I can't win for losing with that woman.

"Okay Mrs. Blaque its in, and the contractions look to be getting a little closer together, so when you fell like you have to, then just push." The doctor said as he removed his hand from my wife. I had to look away. Even though he was a doctor, it still made me uncomfortable as hell.

"So how you feeling baby?" I asked my wife.

"Right now I'm alright I guess, I'm just really thirsty that's all. It's like I got a cotton mouth."

"I'll get you something." I said as I happily walked out of that tight, tense ass room.

I could feel the eyes of Mia's parents following me out the door, and I could hear them wish that I would just keep walking and never look back. I hate

Mia's parents. I literally hate them. The way they made me feel, the way they made me act around them, I hated who I had to be when they were around. Honestly I think it's jealously. Mr. Jones has hated me from the first time he laid eyes on me. Now granted the first time we met, it was unofficial and very accidental. He walked in on me and Mia in a very compromising position. Actually it was a very difficult position. I don't think Mia can even bend like that anymore. I will never forget that day. Mr. Jones looked me in the eyes, asked me to get decent and meet him outside. I thought I was about to get my ass kicked. Out of respect for the man I did as he asked, I got dressed and went outside on the front porch. Mr. Jones was sitting on a big ass wicker chair smoking a fat cigar. I wouldn't doubt it if he had sprinkled some weed in that thing.

He looked like the type to puff and not pass. He motioned for me to sit on the bench next to him. Then he looked at me, puffed his cigar and asked me what I wanted from his daughter. At the time I wanted to tell him the truth. "I had run the race, jumped the tallest hurdles and reached my goal already sir, but thanks for asking." Then just walk away into the sunset, but I didn't. I told Mr. Jones that all I wanted from his daughter was her love. At the time I must say that was a big pile of shit, but hey what do you expect I was young and had just released all my pimp juice, so I was cool, calm and collected.

After I let Mr. Jones know how I felt, he just stared at me. Then after about two minutes of silence he got his fat ass up, started to walk into the house, then turned and said, "If you hurt my daughter in any way, shape or form I will kill you." And with those words left to linger in the smoke filled air, he walked into the house.

"Nigga please! Kill me." I demanded.

Of course I said it to myself as I walked away from his home. Hoping I would never have to return to that house again. I mean, Mia was cool, but I wasn't into the whole relationship thing. That just wasn't me. I could careless if I ever talked to that damn girl again. Or so I thought. The next week in class Mia walked in looking finer then ever. Her glasses had turned into contacts, her loose fitting clothes got a little bit tighter, and the hair that use to cover her face was slicker than a pimps on the first of the month. Damn I guess after you bust a few nuts in a row, you begin to let your hair down. I'm not one to toot my own horn, but Mia came like four or five times in a row that day. Beating my personal goal of three. So Toot Toot!

"Lookin good Mia!" I heard some raggity thug yell Mia's way.

"So when is you gone make time for me in yo busy schedule?"

I had to hear this. That dirty mofo was not Mia's type at all. I was. A man like me, someone that was clean, and could speak proper English, I was her type.

"Here's my number, call me and I'll see when I can fit you in." Mia said as she handed this bum a little piece of paper that held her private number.

"Aight baby I see you, I'ma call you too! "

"Since when is that thug your type? I thought you liked them at least house trained." I said after breaking my silence.

"He looks real, and I like a man who is real. You know what I'm saying El? Someone that won't feed me bullshit lines just because he thinks that's what I want to hear."

"Are you trying to say something Tamia?" I asked as I followed her to her next class.

"I heard what you told my father. That shit about all you want from me is love. That was wack El. Why can't you just be real, my father is a man just like you. I know what you wanted from me, it was the same thing I wanted from you. Some ass! Plain and simple."

I couldn't believe this girl. She straight used me for some ass. I had never been used before.

"Oh like that Mia, is that how you want to play me? Don't sell yourself short baby, I did want a little bit more from you then just ass, I mean a little head would have been nice too."

I know it was wrong, but she just told me she

used me. That shit kinda hurt.

"Whatever El, all I'm saying is you should have been real with my father, and with me. Feeding me all the garbage about wanting to get to know me better, and acting all interested in my future goals. That shit was a waste, I could have kept my thoughts for someone who really cared." She said as she sat on the bench outside of Goodman Hall.

"Mia I did, I mean do care. You seem real cool, but I'm just not into the whole girlfriend boyfriend thing. That's just not me right now." I looked Mia in the eyes and said, "But I was being real with your father, about wanting nothing but love from you, I mean not now but in the future I could see myself with someone like you."

"Thanks El, I'll be sure to put *'falling in love with Elongai'* in my planner, right next the day hell freezes over!"

And with that she walked away, and right into my heart. I know it sounds stupid, but I never had a woman, use me, diss me and walk away from me all in one day. Tamia Jones was a chase that I was up to. This was a game I had to win, and in the end I did.

"You can do it baby!" I said as I fed my wife crushed ice cubes and toweled off her sweaty forehead.

"Alright Mrs. Blaque about three more pushes

to go and you should have your self a brand new baby!" The doctor said a little too overly excited.

Within minutes I heard the most beautiful sound you could ever imagine. My sons cries. I was overjoyed and under prepared for his arrival. I cut the cord, and watched the blood squirt out as I separated my son from his mother. As I held my son in my arms for the first time, I went deaf. I couldn't hear Mia's parents complaining about something I was doing wrong, I couldn't hear Mia's friends chit chatting on how they couldn't wait until it was their turn to pop out a little one of their one. All I could hear were my sons heartbeats as he lay against my chest. I closed my eyes and said a silent prayer for my son, Laurence Jackson Blaque. No matter how badly I wanted to have a Junior, I couldn't live with myself if I named my son Elongai.

His first name, Laurence, is my middle name. His middle name Jackson is Mia's fathers name. I could have done without that, but like I was told its not about me. Finally after about two hours of guests coming and going, it was our time. Family time for the first time. I sat in that hard ass uncomfortable hospital chair next to Mia's bed. She was rubbing Laurence's back through the incubator. He was doing pretty good after being about one month premature, but the doctors still wanted to keep an eye on him. I held my wife's hand and looked into her eyes and said, " I love you Mia." I was in awe. A life just came out of my woman, a living breathing being just slid out of my wife. I feel in love all over again. This was the beginning of a new life, and I welcomed it with open arms.

Andrea

Okay it has been almost two weeks and that fool Javonte hasn't called me back yet. I mean if you don't want to talk to me then let me know. Cause I am not the one to be sitting by the phone waiting okay! I have a life you know. Not a very active life lately, but damnit it's a life. These past two weeks have been the weirdest, slowest, someone please pinch me I hope I'm dreaming kind of weeks. First to start off my week from hell Raheem flips the script on me and tells me not to contact him. What the hell? Then one of my best friends has a baby and calls everyone and their step momma before she even calls me. By the time I got there all of Mia's stuck up model friends where leaving the room.

They got to see my God son before I did. What kind of shit is that? I had a mind to bless her little soul, but I didn't. There is something about a woman that just pushed out eight pounds that says, "Don't fuck with me!" And so I didn't. Plus my girl looked so happy. I was happy too. Ever since I can remember Mia has wanted a family. And just like Lola, what Mia wants Mia gets. When we were in High School and Mia wanted this fine brotha named El. Mia got El. When Mia got her licence and wanted the flyest ride. Mia's parents got her a Navigator. A big ass Navigator! And when Mia wanted to get married and start a family, well Mia got that too. I know it may sound like I'm a little envious of Mia but I'm not. I loved pulling into the High School parking lot and parking my 1987 bucket next to her brand new Navigator. I was thrilled. Tamia and I are best friends and I love her to death, it's just that I had to work extra hard for half of what was given to her. But everything happens for a reason right.

"So Mia how are you feeling?"

I decided to call Mia and see how she was, plus I wanted to hear all the details about the birth. Ever since we were kids we would talk about how it would feel to give birth. We would even act like we gave birth whenever we got a new doll. I know I'm not a kid anymore, but I still want to know if we were close.

"Hey Drea, I'm doing okay, Im feeling a lot more comfortable than I was last week. Girl my little cat was throbbing something awful, if it wasn't for the stitches, El would have been petting that thing down okay."

"Dang Mia like that. I thought you lose your sex drive after you give birth, what the hell is wrong with you, talking bout having El give your kitty a rub down."

This shouldn't surprise me at all. Mia has always been the freak of the week, I guess popping a human out won't stop her juices from flowing.

"No Drea I mean like a massage, not like a

freaky massage. Girl sex is the last thing on my mind right now, plus the doctor said we have to wait about three months before we can do anything."

"How does El feel about that?"

I knew how El was. That was my boy, but he could be such a dog at times. I swear it had to be his looks that attracted Mia to him. Cause his charm was nonexistent.

"Shit he better be okay with it, I just gave his ass a son, and a baby momma all in one."

I had to laugh at that one, it was very rare that Mia's little jokes were ever remotely funny.

"Your crazy girl. So how is that little boy doing? I can't wait to come and see him again."

"He's doing good, he doesn't cry as much as we expected him to, but I doubt that will last. By the way Andrea, Me and El were on our way back from picking up some more diapers. I swear this boy shits more than El and I put together. I don't know where he got that from. Anyways, I saw your Mom today on 26th over in North Minneapolis. What was she doing over there?"

What the hell was my Mom doing over on 26th? Now we live over in North Minneapolis near 26th but why would she be on 26th. You see 26th is the hot spot. Nobody but drug dealers and undercover cops paid off by the drug dealers hang out on that damn block. This was not good, either she's selling drugs on the side, or my sister is back on that shit. Most likely its option number two. My older sister Trina. I love her because she is my sister and I have to, but truthfully speaking, I hate that bitch. She put my family through so much. Smoking that shit. I swear if she's back on that shit, I'm beating her black ass. Damn crack head. Family or not she is gonna always be a crack head to me. That might sound wrong, but that bitch stole my car, television, DVD player, PS2 and my wigs, all in the name of that white devil. Damn!

"Maybe one of the teens over at the center lives over there, or maybe she was asking for directions, shit I don't know, why you asking me like I know why she was over there. Am I my mother's keeper? No, I don't think so. I don't keep her in my pocket, she is a grown ass woman she can go where she wants to go. Why you all up in her business anyways? Don't you and El got better things to do like change some diapers? Why yall gotta be all up in my families business. Who you tell Mia huh? Who else you tell that you seen my Mom over there?"

Even thinking about that made me all jumpy and suspicious like I was the one smoking that shit. My palms started sweating, my leg started shaking and my head was killing me. I felt like the hulk or something, like I was about to change into the crack hoe killer and go hunt my sister down.

"Andrea is everything okay? I asked you one little question and you just went off. You know I ain't tell nobody I saw your Mom over there. Besides even if I did we all know your Mom ain't using that shit. It's Trina I'm worried about. I heard from El's friend Derrick that he saw Trina down at the club shaking.."

I didn't even what to hear the rest of that sentence. I had to cut her off before I heard something I wasn't ready for.

"Mia why are your husband's friends talking about my sister and where she be at? That shit ain't cool Mia. Not at all. Look I gotta go. Kiss my God son for me. I'll holla at you later."

I had to hang up on Mia. I know she didn't mean any harm by it, but she should know how I am about my damn sister. These last two weeks have been crazy and to top it all off, my family is keeping a secret from me. I know something is up with Trina. I swear I hate being the baby of the family. It's like no matter how old you are, or how many grey hairs you have, not that I have any, but If I did I would still get treated like the damn baby. Which is cool when its time to give gifts, cause the baby gets the most. But it's not cool when there is some real shit going on and no one will talk to you about it cause they think you can't handle it. That is the worst feeling in the world when your family treats you like an outsider. But I'm gonna find out what's really going on.

"Hey Momma whatchu doing?"

"I'm working Andrea what do you want?"

I loved my Mom but sometimes I swear she can make you hate her. She got one of those attitudes that people run from. It's like PMS 24/7. But I can careless about an attitude, she better get over whatever it is that is bothering her and act like she's happy to hear from me.

"Looka here Momma I'm not your enemy. I'm your loving, caring, beautiful daughter. I was just calling to see how you were doing and to see what you were having for dinner tonight?"

"Why Andrea? Are you asking to come over and have dinner with me? If you are just ask, I can't stand when you do that, if you want something just ask. Damn. I ain't got time to play these games with you girl I'm too.."

I had to cut her off.

"Momma please! What time is dinner?"

"At six Andrea, and don't be bringing none of your damn nappy headed classmates over, cause I ain't trying to feed no army."

"Okay Momma I'll see you then, Love you."

"Yeah whatever. I meant what I said, don't be bringing nobody here with you. I got just enough for who I love, and you. No outsiders you hear."

Oh Moms got jokes huh? That means she is having an alright day. Which is good, maybe now it won't be so hard to get the story out of her. It's so sad I have to beg for the 411 on my family, but that's life I guess. My life.

"I heard you the first time bye Mother!"

My mom and I aren't that close, we never were and I doubt we ever will be. We have one of those tell-tell type of relationships. I tell her what's going on with my life and she tells me what to do with it. Most people would see her as controlling, but I know it comes from the heart so I don't trip. Besides all her advice seems to work. Be it with school, work or relationships her advice always works. She is the one who taught me how to deal with men, and with Raheem. See I used to look at men like they were high and mighty. Like they were the Method Man to my Mary, like they were all I needed to get by. I guess I looked up to men because I thought they were all like my father. My mother took that idea out of my head with the quickness.

I never really knew my father, from what I can remember he was a good man. He died when I was six years old. My mother told me he was in Africa helping build new schools and churches. She says that it was during one of the not so uncommon genocides over there that my father was killed. She doesn't really give me too much detail, but I did know he died while helping others. That's the only image of a man I had. My father the humanitarian. A good man. My mom taught me that my father was a good, yet rare man. And after dealing with Raheem I started to believe her. But tonight we weren't gonna be discussing my life, we were going to be talking about what the hell she was doing on that hot ass block. I'm sick of being left in the dark when shit goes down. Tonight I'm gonna get the respect I deserve, and someone is gonna tell me what the hell is going on.

El

"He looks just like you man. He got your eyes, your funny looking noise, and those ashy ass lips of yours!" Raheem said laughing at his own joke.

"Ha ha Raheem, your just mad cause now you got more competition to worry about, ugly negro!"

We laughed. It felt so good to laugh again. It's been almost three weeks since Mia had our son, and she has been tripping. I don't know if it's that depression that women get after the baby, or if she just has a problem with me. Now that I think about it, it might be me. Usually if there was something going on, if someone was mad, it was me. I was always the one mad at Mia because she wouldn't act like a wife. Don't get me wrong, I'm not one of those types of men. Not at all, but damn I'm a man first and a husband second anyway you look at it. But this time it wasn't Mia that wasn't treating me right, it was me not treating my wife like she was my wife.

I love my wife to death, don't get me wrong, but sometimes she can get on my last nerve. I don't really know why. I mean maybe it's the baby. Maybe it's because our sleep pattern is way off, maybe it's because most nights she sleeps with the baby. I don't know. This might sound like a big deal, but I have been here before with Mia. When we first got together, I was a dog, straight up and down. But after a while I got kinda soft, and she got used to it. But now my dog is coming back. And that un-welcomed comeback is starting to show. I'm not even sure she notices anyways. I mean she spends so much time with our son, it's like I don't exist anymore until she needs something. And excuse my French but, fuck that. I'm no part-time lover. I'm sure this is nothing big, just going through the motions. This too shall pass.

"You're a lucky man El." Raheem said.

"Lucky to have a son. But I'm not sure that luck rubbed off when it came to having a wife though."

Raheem hated when I talked about my wife like I didn't appreciate her. It's not that I don't appreciate her, but it's just a lot going on in my head right now. And Mia and her female issues are not a priority to me, not right now.

"Look at you man. A family man. I would have never guessed this would be you before me. You seem so into yourself and your business, I would have never thought in a million years it would be you with a kid before me." He said changing the subject.

Raheem was right about the whole having a family thing. This really isn't my thing. It's his. He would always be the one talking about having a wife, kids and a house. He was the family man, and I was just the plain ole' man. Me and Raheem are so different it's amazes me that we are as close as we are.

He probably would have had a family started by now if he would be a man about his. I love my boy, but he is whipped, and on what I don't know cause his girl ain't gave him none. Not ever. Hasn't even let the head have a peak. That's just wrong, how much can a man take? Well let me rephrase that, how much can that man take? All I know is, it couldn't be me.

"Yeah I hear you bro, but this could easily be you with a family of your own. I already told you what to do. Tell Andrea like it is. Tell her, 'Look girl, I'm a man with needs and you as my woman no matter what your beliefs, need to be there for me and fulfill every single one of them.' Period. Then let her cry, shit let her yell, and when she calms down escort her ass into the bedroom and beat it up! You got how many years built up in you?"

"Too many. About four and a half years of no ass, no head, shit and barely no palm. Not even a sneak peak. Looking back it sounds stupid, but there is something there. Something deeper than sex."

Oh no here we go. This brotha knows he is too shallow to try to be so deep. Ain't shit deeper then sex, but some better sex, and deeper than that is some great sex. Need I go on? That's one of the main reasons I love Mia so much. She knows how to put it down. When I want it, I get it. And when I don't get it, well lets just say no matter her mood, I get it.

"Brotha, I don't know what that girl has done to you. You're whipped. I can't say your pussy whipped, cause negro you ain't got none. So what? Are you mind whipped? Personality whipped? Is Andrea that deep of a person? What is it man? I don't get why you haven't stepped out on her and got you some. Ain't nothing wrong with having a little creep until your girl acts right. Shit it's not like you're married."

"I love her man. Simple as that. You know before Andrea I could get it whenever I wanted it, but that shit gets old El. It got real old. I was looking for something real, someone that I could build with. Andrea was that one, is that one. She has everything that I was lacking from every other chick. With them the sex was there, but that was it. I didn't long to hear their voice, unless it was screaming my name. But with Andrea I long for all of her, even without the sex, I long for her. That's why I haven't stepped out on her, been there done that."

"Raheem did you forget who you were talking to? It's me El. Mia is not here, you ain't gotta worry about her coming in here and hearing you talk about her girl. It's just me and you bro. So be real. I know for a fact that you have done your dirt behind Drea's back. I'm not going to tell Mia, if that's what you're worried about. I just have to know man. Cause I'm starting to worry about you. No ass in almost five years. That is not natural for any man. You feel me?"

"El, the fact is, I'm in love. I would never cheat on Andrea. Ever. Even though we may have our problems, I would never hurt her like that. She deserves a lot more."

"And you deserve some ass. Period point blank." I said as I watched Raheem's high yellow hue turn pink.

He had the nerve to get mad over this. Even though I knew he wouldn't admit it, I knew my boy was mad. I'm not sure if he was mad at me for my comments, or if I hit the nail on the head, and he had begun to realize that I was speaking the truth. Whatever it was, it had him damn near red with anger. I knew it wasn't going to come to blows, or even an arguing match, but I did see I had hit a nerve.

"I feel you bro." He said with a long pause that had me contemplating my next move. I needed to change the subject, cause I could see the lack of ass was making him all emotional like a damn female.

"But that's where we differ I guess." He finally finished.

"So how is your Mom doing? I haven't heard from her in a couple of months."

"Oh yeah she's doing good, real good. She got her self a new man. You know I'm not feeling that whole situation. Got this grown man staying up in my house, eating my fruit loops and shit."

Raheem was defiantly one of a kind. Only he, a grown ass man himself, would get mad cause his Mom got a man living with her. The man in me wanted to tell him, 'Negro you ain't no better, at least your Moms getting something from the man, you ain't even helping her out with the rent.' But the friend in me softened that blow.

"She is a grown ass woman herself, I mean she got to have her life too. Let Stella get her groove back, and worry about where your going to be employed at. You know I got an open position at the company. It's been almost six months since you were laid-off. Make your next move your best move."

Ever since I got that business loan from the bank, I have been trying to get Raheem to work for me, or with me as he likes to put it. But he won't bite. Like my Grandmother used to say, "You can lead a horse to water, but you can't make it swim." Or something like that. The point is I'm trying to help my boy out with some income coming in, but for some odd reason he would rather be broke than work for me.

"I hear you El. I really do." There it was again, another long pause. "Well I'm gonna be heading out. It was real. Tell Mia I said what's up." And with that he got up, kissed my son on the head, gave me a chin up and walked toward the door. Then he turned and said, "Your blessed El, you really are, don't be so rough on Mia. I know how you can get, just know your blessed. Don't let your ego mess this up."

As I closed the door behind him, his words lingered in the air. He was right. For once or maybe twice in my life, I was wrong. The way I was treating Mia was wrong. Even if she didn't notice it, I was thinking things I shouldn't have been thinking. I was saying things I shouldn't have been saying. I was demanding things I shouldn't have been demanding. Even though this woman just had my son I still excepted head at least twice a day, and even with tears in her eyes she did what she had to do to make me happy. I was wrong. Raheem was right. I am blessed. I guess it was time I started thinking about more than just myself. I looked down at my son, and seen an image of me. It gave me the chills. I didn't want my son to become what I had turned into. As I closed my eyes, a tear fell onto my son's face while he slept. I said a prayer to be a better man. It was time for me to be a better man, even though I thought I already was. It was worth a try.

Raheem

I really wasn't trying to hear El preach to me about getting ass. He really needed to understand that we do things differently. El might be the type to take ass without a second thought about the person he was taking it from. I'm over that. I don't want to take anymore. I want to receive it. Sex is better when its given to you freely. No games, no strings, just good ole' love making. And with how long it's been since I had some, I would welcome it with open arms. El had a point. This shit ain't natural for any man. Almost five years. Love can make you do some crazy shit. Lord knows I love Andrea with all my heart. I love her because she loves me. It might sound weak of me, but it's the truth. Her type of love is what I needed. She encourages me in a way that shows me she really cares. That alone is a wonderful thing. I just really wish she could see how much she means to me.

I tried my hardest to show her. Like when she told me she was a virgin and wasn't ready for sex, I gave her time. I just didn't know that would turn into four and a half years. Whenever she needed her space, I gave it to her. Even when I knew she would talk to other cats, I still let her go. Our love is like a boomerang, no matter how long we might be away we always found our way back to each other. Well I used to believe that. But the way things are going, I feel like it's all a game to her. I can't really say I'm being used, cause I ain't got shit to be used for. But something about this break up didn't feel right to me. Usually she would call me and make sure I'm okay, or send me some cutesy little card telling me how much she loves me. It's like every time I think I can move on, or I start to let go, she shows up, and I fall again. Harder each time. That's why I told her not to do that shit this time. I feel if you want to break up with me, then let's do it right. No bullshit. No games.

Plus the reason for breaking up with me was bogus as hell. She knew I wasn't a bum. I'm just going through some things right now. I had a good job, making good money, but they downsized, and so did my income. Unemployment ain't shit, don't let anybody fool you. Then I had to sell my truck just to pay my rent. Then I got a notice that my rent was going up, I couldn't find a decent job to keep up with the increase so I had to move out. I had to come back home with my Mom. How do you think that shit made me feel? A twenty five year old man living back at home. I felt like a good for nothing bum, and I really didn't need to hear my girl tell me what I already knew. What I needed was for her to tell me everything was going to be alright. I needed her to have my back when shit got real.

But instead she turned her back on me, and that hurts like hell. I might not be the best man, but I am a good man. I would give Andrea anything she needed, but that just wasn't enough. Right now I don't know where we stand. I'm not sure if I'm ready to move on, or if she's moving on. I'm not sure of anything anymore. I don't do shit all day, but think about Andrea. I need a hobby, shit I need a job. Times like this I wish I had never left the University just because I got that job. I thought I had made it. And for a while I had, but then like Kanye says, "It All Falls Down." And it fell hard.

"Who is it?" I yelled at the front door. I wasn't excepting anyone, and my Mom and her new "friend" were out of town.

"It's me." I heard a little voice whisper.

"Who the hell is Mee, Don't know Mee live here. I think you might want the Yangs next door, I'm sure there is a Mee, You and Who over there." I know that was wrong, but damn I was on my way to bed.

"Its Mia Raheem. Mia."

"Oh my bad girl." I said as I ran to the door to let her in.

I was hoping she had my God son with her, but when I opened the door the only bundle I saw was the twenty or more Kleenexes she had in her hands.

"What's going on Mia?"

"I tried to call Andrea but she won't answer my

calls, My parents are out of town at some convention, and El.." She stopped and started to cry like someone had died.

"El what Mia, is El alright? What's going on? Come in here and have a seat."

I damn near had to carry her over to the couch and sit her down myself. I didn't know what was going on, but whatever it was, it wasn't good.

"El wont let me in." Mia said through her tears.

"What do you mean he wont let you in Mia? What are you talking about? It's nearly four below outside, why would your husband lock you out?"

The more I asked to more the answer became clear to me. But just like Mia, I wasn't trying to see it. El could be the nicest man on earth, but with the flip of a switch he would change the game. He only did that when he was going through something, but I had just left from there and he seemed alright to me.

"Its okay Mia, its gonna be okay."

What was gonna be okay? I didn't even know what she was talking about, but it sounded good. That's what I would want to be told if I was as hysterical as she was.

"Why is he like this Raheem? Why would he shut me out like this? I'm no dummy I can't tell when something is not right, and Raheem something is not right. I know you know what going on. If he won't tell me then you have to." Mia demanded.

Okay. This was really starting to piss me off, what the hell was she talking about. Enough talking in codes, I had to know what she was talking about.

"Mia calm down, and explain what's going on?"

"El wont let me touch him. At all. Just out the blue, he was like, 'I'm not in the mood for that right now.' I'm no fool. He is always in the mood for some head. He even made me a schedule after the baby came for when he wanted it, and I was always right on time. One night we had got into a big ass argument, I mean I was screaming and crying, it was some real emotional shit. Then right in the middle of it his alarm went off and he was like, 'You know what time it is, wipe those eyes and go to work.' So I know something is up if my own husband out of the blue tells me he don't want any head action from his wife. It's not like I don't know what I'm doing or anything. You should see how your boy acts when I.."

This was entirely too much information. I started to feel nauseous because I had a visual. What have I gotten myself into?

"Mia I thought you said he won't let you in. Why did he lock you out the house?"

"He didn't lock me out the house Raheem. I mean he wont talk to me about what's going on in his head. How does someone just switch like that if everything is okay? Something is not right. I can feel it. He tried to make it like it had nothing to do with me, but I know it does. He doesn't find me attractive anymore does he Raheem?"

She asked as the water works began to fall once again. I didn't say anything, I just held her, and let her cry. I didn't know what was going on with the two of them, and I didn't know if it was my business to try to find out. All I knew was that Mia was hurting, and I just wanted to make it right. I don't even know why she would think that El doesn't find her attractive anymore. No disrespect to my boy but Mia was fine. Always has been and by looking at how the years have treated her lately, she always will be.

"Mia, El's just stressed over business. It has nothing to do with you. I'm sure. I was just over there, and he was telling me how in love he is with you, and how he felt so blessed when it came to his family. Especially his wife."

I was making it up as I talked, but she needed to hear this right now. It wasn't the place or the time for the truth. Not that I would even know the truth if it jumped out a Cadillac and pimp slapped me. But what I did know was that something was up with El, I just didn't know what.

"Then if its just stress why won't he talk to me about it?"

"You know how El is Mia. He wants to deal with it alone. Trust me it's nothing big, and it definitely has nothing to do with you. You're perfect in his eyes. Everything is perfect. He is just trying to make more time for his family right now. He feels like he hasn't been doing his job as a father and as a husband. Its hard hiring new folks to help out with his business, but that's what he is gonna have to do in order to spend more time with you. Hiring is stressful Mia, just trust me. Everything is going to work out fine."

There, I was officially the worst liar in America. What the hell was I talking about? Shit I don't even know. I just hope Mia bought it.

"So does that mean your gonna work with us and help out! It would be a lot less stressful if you came and worked with us, it's like we kill two birds with one stone. Now El won't be stressed about hiring someone he doesn't really know, and you can help out when El is spending time with Laurence and me." Mia said as she looked up at me with her puffy red eyes.

She sounded so happy, I didn't want to burst her little joy bubble, but I couldn't work with El. Even though I know he needs the help, and I could make some real good money. The thing is you don't work with El, you work for El. I love him like a brother, but El is a control freak, and I'm not trying to have a grown man controlling me. I just can't do it. But Mia looked so happy, and so at ease. I guess it wouldn't be that bad. I would have a job, have a car in no time, and eventually Andrea. Actually this isn't a bad idea after all.

"Drive safely!" I yelled out to Mia as she hopped oh so happily into her Mercedes LS. Now I just had to fill El in on my little conversation with Mia before she got home.

Andrea

"Eight missed calls! " I said to myself as I checked my messages.

I had left my phone in my car while I was at my Moms house. After I realized all the missed calls where from Mia, and not one of them was from Raheem or Javonte I didn't feel that special. I wonder what the hell she called me so many times for.

"Drea it's me, Mia, I hope you're not avoiding my calls on purpose cause I really need to talk to you. Dang! El wont talk to me, my parents aren't around, and you won't pick up. I'm on my way to Raheems house. I need to talk to someone. Call me when you can."

What's going on? I was hoping Mia was just spazzing out over nothing. After I talked to her, I realized that's exactly what it was. I love Mia, she is my girl and all, but damn she creates more drama then a Jerry Springer producer. I know one day El is gonna get sick of that shit. Who am I kidding? El ain't going anywhere and neither is Mia. Those love birds make me sick. Plus I got my own drama to worry about.

After I told my Mom I was coming over, I guess she got the clue that I had heard about Trina, so she called Trina over to the house. When I walked in the door, I almost passed out. I seen my Mom and my sister sitting at the piano playing and singing together like everything was alright. I'm not stupid. No matter how much makeup or perfume you throw on a crack head, their gonna always be a damn crack head.

"Doesn't Trina look good Andrea?" My mother asked me.

"I guess. What is she doing here? Are we having another intervention or something? Cause if we are I got better things to do with my time."

"Andrea Denise don't come in my house and disrespect your family like that. Trina is your blood, but you treat her like some bum off the street. We are family, and we stick together though thick or thin. Your sister has cleaned up her act, tell her Trina." My Mother said as she nudged Trina to talk to me.

"I haven't used in two months sis!" She said through a phoney smile. I'm nobody's fool, family or not, I had to speak my damn mind.

"So what you want Trina, an award for acting like a responsible woman? Please! Your not getting any praise from me for doing what you're suppose to be doing. So what you've been clean for two months. Big freaking deal. I heard this all before Trina. I know you, you might be older than me but you damn sure ain't wiser."

"Watch your mouth girl. What did I tell you about disrespect in my home? First it was your sister now your disrespecting me? What has gotten into you Andrea?“

My mother spoke with pain in her voice, but at that time I was too self righteous to notice.

“If Trina is clean and all, then why were you on 26th today Momma? If you weren't looking for her then why were you over there? What are you using too?"

I swear I said that in my mind. I didn't mean for that to come out, not like that. My gut told me to hurry up and apologize but before I could even catch my breath.

Wapp!

My mom smacked the shit out of me. I didn't even see her coming. I swear she went from being across the room, sipping on tea. To in my face knocking the taste out my mouth. For a moment I didn't know what to do. My pride soon gave me my instructions. While holding my face, I got up, put on my coat and headed for the door without a word.

"Andrea don't leave!" I heard Trina say.

I turned around, "This is your fault, this whole thing was about you and your stupid addiction. You can fool Momma all you want, but I know you Trina. This won't last for long."

I closed the door behind me and walked to my car. It was so icy out that before I could get to my car, I fell flat on my ass. I was already furious and that fall just added to my anger. I finally made it to my car and hopped inside and started it up. I had to warm it up before I went anywhere. Before I could turn on my music, I heard a tapping noise at my window.

"What do you want Trina?" I yelled at my sister from inside my car.

"Open the door Andrea!", Trina said as she wiped the tears from her eyes before they froze to her face. It was cold has hell.

I opened the door. Something inside of me told me not to let her in. I should have listened to my gut. Little did I know I was letting her into more then just my car.

"We need to talk Andrea. We are family, and you shouldn't be treating me like this. Talking down to me in front of Momma, you know that ain't right. Do you think your Miss Perfect or something? Well you're not. You ain't better than me Andrea. You did your dirt back in the day, so don't try to make it like I'm this big drug user when that's not even the story."

I have to be in the twilight zone or something. Am I on Candid Camera? This is too funny. The nerve of my sister, and I use that word loosely. How dare she get her funky ass in my car and start pointing fingers. Trying to make me out to be the bad guy was not going to work. I knew her game, her crack head logic was not going to work on me. Not again, not this time.

"Trina who do you think your talking too? I'm not the crack head, you are. I didn't steal my sister's shit for that white devil, you did. So what maybe I tried weed once or twice, that don't make me a fiend like you. That makes me normal. You on the other hand, that stuff has turned you out, it pimped you. Look at you Trina. You're hooked on that shit. I can tell, maybe Momma can't, but I can. Your hair is thinning out, your breath smells like death and your skin looks like it belongs on someone twice your age."

My sister used to be so beautiful, and if you squinch your eyes and look at her through a foggy mirror she still was. She is a little bit lighter than me, but everyone still considers her dark skinned. Her hair was long and curly. I guess the Indian kicked in for her and skipped me. Trina could have been a model I swear. Well maybe not, she was pretty short. About 5'4. Used to be a cute little thing, but not anymore. I have to admit though, she has cleaned up just a little bit from the last time I saw her. This was the first time I saw my sister in almost three months. No matter how hard I may act, it hurt to see my sister strung out like that. I had to stay away.

"I'm not here to argue with you sis. All I wanted

to do was show you that I had cleaned my act up. You don't have to believe me Andrea, and I know you don't. I will show you how I have changed. Not just on the outside, but on the inside too. Sis' I found God, and he showed me the light. He showed me that everything I was doing wasn't in my steps."

I don't think I laughed that hard in a while.

"Oh Trina thank you girl, I needed that laugh I really did. You found God? Get the hell out my car. Now!"

I can't take anymore. I wanted to believe her I really did, but it was something in my gut that told me not to.

"I'm serious sis. I really am. You know me I know you do, but look at me." I did as she asked.

"I might not be the best person, but don't let my past take my future away. I am really trying. I just need my family to support me. That is all I'm asking is for you to just be there for me."

Her crack head logic was starting to sound a little too reasonable to me. Throughout all the, "let me comeback in you life" tears she has cried, and through all the lies she has told, I actually believed her this time. Something about her eyes told me she was trying.

"Trina I swear to your new found God, if you

put our family through anymore bullshit, I will personally kick your ass. Do you hear me?"

Even though I was younger than she was, she still treated me like I was the older sister. So in turn I acted like one.

"I hear you sis. I just need one chance to make it right with yall, I won't let you down, I swear I wont." Trina said as she hugged me.

I reluctantly hugged her back. I was really split on how I should feel. Was I supposed to always have faith in my sister, because she was family, or was I supposed to always keep in the back of my mind all the drama she has put me through? I wasn't sure how to feel or how to act. For the first time in a long time I was at a loss for words.

"So can we go back in the house so you and Mom can make up?"

"Shit I might get knocked out again!" I said jokingly as we walked back into the house.

There was my Mom, sitting at the piano, singing like she was Alicia Keys or somebody. My Mom reminded me of the mother on The Cosby's. She always had on some colorful silky outfit. She was from the hood, but at times would talk like she was raised in the burbs. My mom was a teen counselor at the local community center. Funny huh? She had all the advice in the world for the teens in the neighborhood, but when it came to her own kids, she let her hands do the talking.

Don't get me wrong, she didn't beat us for no reason. Oh no. We were some bad ass kids. I just wish she would have talked to us the way she talks to those kids. With Trina and me, my Mom didn't talk to us, she just whipped our bad ass's, then sent us to our room. She wouldn't talk to us for a couple of days, then out the blue she would act like everything was okay. I don't know if that's how she was raised or what, but as she can see by looking at Trina, that shit doesn't work.

"Andrea, honey you know I didn't mean to hit you like that."

"I know Momma. I'm sorry for disrespecting you." I said as I gave her a hug and sat down next to her on the piano bench. I couldn't play to save my life, but I loved listening to my Mother play.

"So did you and your sister talk Andrea?"

"Yes we did. Trina told me she was serious about cleaning up her act this time and I believe she can do it this time Momma." I said half way lying.

"I know Andrea. I'm really proud of your sister. She was telling me about how she found a job as a waitress at a restaurant outside of town. She goes to church and everything. She is really trying. I can tell. Hopefully she won't need to stay at your place for longer than a month or two."

Who? What? Where? When? You have got to be kidding me. This is the reason why I am such a bitch. Don't just volunteer my place out as Rehab America. Oh hell no!

"What are you talking about? Who said anything about Trina moving in with me? Why can't one of her church folk friends help her out?"

"Because we are family Andrea Denise."

I had to really watch my words now. Whenever my Mom called me by my first and middle name, I knew she wasn't taking any shit.

"Momma I understand that, but why couldn't we, meaning you and me, why couldn't we talk about this first. Why would yall just make plans that include me, without me? I don't understand how that works. Is anyone going to ask me if I'm okay with having Trina move in with me? Do I at least get that much?"

I glared at my sister just sitting there with nothing to say. She was weak, letting Mom do the talking for her. Shit if you want a favor from somebody, you ask. Grow up. Trina knew exactly what I was thinking.

"Sis' I don't have to stay with you. I can stay where I've been staying. No big deal."

"Sounds good to me. Now that, that's settled what's for dinner?"

"Settled hell Andrea! Your sister is not going to continue living in that crack house. I was just over there today getting the rest of her stuff. That is the reason I was over there. What's wrong with you? Care enough about your sister to at least help her out for a couple of months. I shouldn't even have to ask you to look out for your sister. You should be offering. I bet if one of your little friends needed help you wouldn't hesitate to offer."

I could feel the storm approaching. I saw the clouds forming. Heard the thunder roaring, the lighting was striking and I was flying a kite without an umbrella. What was I supposed to do, argue with my Mom and get knocked out? I don't think so. If I said no then I was going to be made out to be the bad guy, but if I said yes then I was going to have to deal with Trina's crack head tendencies. Whether she was clean or not, those tendencies don't go away.

"Your right, I'm sorry. Trina, I'm sorry. You can come stay with me for as long as you need to, but this won't be a free ride by any means. You get your own food, and you will pay half of everything that you use."

I highly doubt that she could even pay attention, let alone pay me rent. But the control was taken away from me when this decision was made without me. I had to have the upper hand some way.

"Okay sis, I understand. Whatever I need to do I will. This is a new day for me."

It might have been a new day for her, but it felt like a freaking nightmare to me. My gut told me to just say no and be the bad guy for once, but once again I didn't listen to my gut. My gut has never failed me before, I was just hoping this time it was wrong.

El

I don't know what's wrong with my wife. If I tell her to touch me, she sucks her teeth and rolls her eyes, but when I tell her its okay she doesn't have to touch me, she still gets upset. I can't win with this woman. After the talk I had with Raheem I realized how I was treating my wife. Making a schedule for her to show me love. That wasn't right. It felt right, but it wasn't right. I don't know where she ran off too. Hopefully she went to talk to Andrea. Most guys can't stand their woman's female friends, but Andrea always has had my back, and I'm not too sure why. It's not that we aren't that close, because we are, but I just have never heard of chick looking out for her friends man.

I was sick of waiting for Mia so I decided to go to the corner store. It was empty as hell in there. I think only about two people were in there, and they were on their way out. Maybe it was so empty because it was so cold out. No one in their right mind would be out in this weather, unless it was some kind of emergency. I wouldn't call trouble at home an emergency, but I just needed to get out of the house. Waiting for Mia was doing a number on my nerves. Walking up and down the aisles would be sure to calm them just a little bit. Hopefully. I shouldn't be so uptight about our little problem, it was far from serious, but the guilt I was feeling was eating me up inside. I grabbed all the comfort food that little hand basket could hold. From Twinkies to a six pack of beer, if it wasn't good for me, it was in my basket.

"I'm gaining weight just looking at all this food!" The clerk said.

I was afraid to look up and begin a short conversation with the clerk. Last time I did that I saw that fool that was in my nightmares. I didn't want to even see his face. He might just pop back in my dreams. I couldn't let that happen. I had enough drama to deal with. Adding this into the mix would not be a good look.

"I was just joking sorry if I offended you sir. Not that you would even have to worry about gaining weight. Being in such good shape must take a lot of time huh?"

Damnit. Don't give me a compliment *and* ask me a question. Now I have to respond.

"Yeah it does take a lot of time, but working out relieves a lot of stress."

"Well maybe I should try working out, stress has become like second nature to me lately."

"You seem too young to be that stressed out." I said warming up to the clerk.

It wasn't as bad as I thought it would be, even

though he was the man in my nightmare. He probably just needed someone to talk to since it was like a ghost town in there. Plus he didn't seem as gay as he was in my dream.

"Yeah well stress don't care how old you are I'll tell you that right now." He said has he packed the last of my bags.

"Maybe you just need to take a break, meditate or something, I need to meditate myself."

"Can I show you something?" He asked.

"Why not?", I said before my thoughts caught up to my words. I had a habit of talking before thinking. A very bad habit.

He looked around, I guess to make sure no one else was in the store. He took his smock off, threw it on the register and came from behind the counter and locked the doors. I don't know why I didn't just grab my bags and go. Not that I was in a rush to get home, but I just felt a little too friendly with this nameless guy.

"I'm Mark. And you are?" He said as I followed him to the back of the store. I felt the aisles getting longer and longer as we walked.

"El. My friends call me El." I said with nervousness in my response.

"Nice to meet you El. You seem pretty cool. I see you in here a lot at night, getting diapers and formula. How many kids do you have?"

"One. Just one. A son. With my wife."

I had to throw that in. Even though he looked more thugged out then a 50 Cent video set, I had to let him know.

"Must be nice. Well here it is." He said as he opened up what looked like a stock room converted into a mini spa.

There was a long table with a white table cloth on it and one of those blow up bath pillows on one end. There were unlit candles all around, about Twenty or so.

"Looks like you have your own little oasis here. Nice set up." I said as I checked out the Feng Sui of this mini spa. Another bad habit of mine. I looked up at the ceiling lights, they were flickering out of control, like the power was about to go out, and knowing my luck they would.

"Damn. This happens almost every night. I'll be right back. I need to go check the breakers." Mark said as he threw me a lighter.

I was assuming he had a feeling the lights were about to go out. After he left, I began to light the candles. I might be a man, but I hate the dark. All of a sudden the lights were out.

"They should be on in a couple of minutes. This happens all the time I'm telling you. You would think they would get this shit fixed." Mark said with anger in his voice. Too much anger, just for some lights going out.

"Scared of the dark?" I said jokingly.

"Hell yeah I'm scared of the dark." I could relate to the seriousness in his voice. I had to laugh.

"I'm sorry I don't mean to laugh, it's just you don't look like the type to be afraid of the dark."

"Looks can be deceiving El, and I'm not afraid of the dark, I just don't like it aight." He said with a smile on his face.

"Yeah aight Mark." He seemed real down to earth.

"So this is your little getaway huh?"

"Yeah, a little somethin, somethin. Try it out, see if it relaxes you."

"What? You want me to get on that make shift massage table, and then what? You gonna play some ocean waves or something? I'm straight."

"Sure you are. Just try it, you said you needed something to relax you. Here you go." Mark said as he led me to the table.

I stood there for a while, not because I didn't hear what he said, but I was just stuck on his comment. "Sure you are." What the hell was that suppose to mean? I'm as straight as an arrow. Who the hell did he think he was to question me?

"What did you mean when you said, sure you are?" I had to know.

"Nothing really, just that your mouth is saying no but your bodies saying yes, that's all. Listen to you tightness El."

"What the fuck are you talking about? My body saying yes?" No man should ever quote R. Kelly to another man. Was this fool coming onto me?

"Chill out man damn. What I mean is stress ain't good for your body, that's all."

I felt kinda stupid.

"Oh I thought you meant that you.. Never mind I was just making sure." I said as I laid on the table.

"The silence is calming huh?" Mark said as he walked toward me.

I began to really relax. All my stress began to melt away. My tight shoulders began to loosen up. I took deep breaths inhaling the incense Mark had lit. Then I felt his hands on my back. Massaging me.

"Ay man what the hell?"

"Relax El, like I said your body needs this." Mark said in a tone that didn't match his thugged out persona. I tried to move away, I tried to get up but I was stuck. I couldn't move. I couldn't speak.

"There you go, just relax. This will take so much stress away it will amaze you."

I felt my shirt being pulled over my head. I saw Mark grab a bottle of baby oil out of his back packet, like he had planned this. What have I gotten myself into, and why couldn't I move? Mark rubbed the oil all over my back, then turned me over.

"You're so stiff." He said with a smirk.

He looked like a little devil. A thugged out devil. I thought he was referring to my tight shoulders being stiff, but when I saw where his eyes where looking I quickly caught his drift. I was at full attention. Why? I cleared my throat. I felt my voice trying to say something. Whatever came out it wasn't gonna be polite.

"Hmmmm." I moaned! It was like I was possessed.

"You like that huh?" Mark said as he rubbed my wife's play thing.

I wanted to leave, I wanted to kick his ass, but I

couldn't move. I was in shock, how could this feel so good. Mark must have felt my hesitation and thought he could make it go away. He leaned in and looked me deep in my eyes. He had deep eyes, I was hypnotized, in a passion filled daze. I gave in. His lips where as soft as Mia's, his tongue was a little too big for my taste. What was I talking about? This was a man! I don't have a taste for men! My thoughts took a while to catch up with my actions, and when they did I pulled away.

"Ring, ring! " Mark said.

"What?" I yelled. What the hell does ring ring mean, is that some gay code.

"Ring, ring!" He yelled at me.

Before I could get up off the table, it disappeared from under me, then the whole room began to fade. Mark must have drugged me. I shut my eyes tight, and rubbed them until it hurt. When I opened them, I saw something that scared me and thrilled me at the same time. I was home. That ringing was from the phone. I passed out on the couch waiting for Mia to come home.

"Hello?" I said hoping it was my wife on the other end.

"Hey bro. Man what the hell is going on over there? You got your wife shook the hell up. She came over here crying and shit. What's up man?

I had to snap back to reality quickly. If Raheem heard even a little shake in my voice, he would want to know why. Speaking of why. Why the hell would Mia go see Raheem? This didn't look right, sound right, it just wasn't right. Now Andrea I could see, but Raheem?

"What do you mean my wife was shook the hell up? Are you and Andrea back together? Is that how you seen her?"

"No she came over my Mom's spot. She said she tried to call Andrea first but she was avoiding her calls or something like that. Shit I don't know, but all I know is, your little attitude spasms got your wife on panic mode. She thinks you don't find her attractive after the baby."

"What. Man what did you tell her Raheem?"

After he told me how it all went down I was surprised at how great of a liar he had became. I must say he cleaned it up pretty nicely.

"Good looking Raheem. So when were you planning on telling me about the job?"

"Look El, I really would like to help you out, and get paid at the same time, but we need some ground rules first."

"Ground rules? What kind of ground rules? Now don't think cause you pacified my wife you can start running shit. Cause that ain't happening."

"Nothing like that El. All I want is to be treated right. I know how you run your camp. You are one controlling mofo."

"Oh I got you. You're my boy Raheem. You don't have to worry about me bossing you around. I trust you don't need me breathing down your back every four minutes."

"Cool. So I guess I'll see you on Monday?"

"Bright and early. I'm glad you finally decided to work with the company."

"Yeah well, your wife kind of made that decision for me, but I'm gonna roll with it."

"Well I'll see you Monday bro. Oh and thanks again for talking to Mia."

"No problem."

Apart of me was relived that Raheem calmed Mia down, but the other half was mad as hell that Mia would talk to my boy about our sex life. She can tell all her little girl friends all she wants, but my boy! Now that's crossing the line. Now I got Raheem looking at me all crazy. Even though he didn't say anything about it, I know what he's thinking. What any man in their right mind is thinking. Why would you turn down sex from your wife? I'm glad Raheem didn't ask too many questions, because I wouldn't quite know how to answer them, especially after that nightmare.

Andrea

"Thanks for coming to help me move this stuff Leaky."

I had called Malik hoping he wasn't busy tonight. I really didn't need help clearing out my office, but I did need the company. I might be seen as a strong female, but truth be told I hate being alone.

"No problem. I was bored as hell sitting at home anyway. I was glad when you called. Now where did you want all this?"

"Into the living room I guess."

I was still kinda upset that I had to get rid of my office for Trina. When I got this two-bedroom apartment, I couldn't wait to turn the second room into an office. It wasn't the best office, but damn it, it was mine. I had a little rickety desk I got from Wal-Mart, with a chair that couldn't hold itself up, let alone me. But it was mine. I had all my awards up on the walls. Honor Roll and shit like that. I haven't done anything too awarding in a while so those awards where pretty old.

"Is that from Kindergarten?" Malik asked as he pointed to one of my awards. I told you they were old.

"Yeah Miss. Webb's class. Remember that?" Malik and I went to the same Elementary and Middle school.

Halfway through our school year he went to another High School in another city straight, and came back gay. Go figure.

"I couldn't stand that heifer. She was so jealous of me. It was ridiculous."

Malik thought everyone was jealous of him. Surprisingly most of the time he was right, and he would bring it up until it got so high he couldn't reach it anymore. But if he was wrong, you dare not mention it ever again. It was a dead subject.

"I can't believe Miss Trina is coming to live with you. Girl I might have to move in this building, cause I know there is gonna be some drama up in here." Malik said as he took down my precious awards.

"I doubt it Malik. Trina knows better than to bring anything other than her ashy ass up in here. I got too much shit going on right now. I don't have time to worry about that grown woman."

"What you got going on Drea? Not a damn thing. Your not going to back to class until next fall, since you need a "break" as you call it. You and that bum ain't together and Javonte is M.I.A. You're not working. So what the hell do you have going on?"

All up in my business.

"First of all Malik I do have a job. I'm working with my homegirl until Fall Semester. And second of all for your information it's an internship, so it's going toward my credits *and* I'm getting paid. And third of all you terd of a man, Javonte is not missing in action, he's just busy with school." Damn him.

"Bitch Boo. That fool is busy alright. Busy with his girl."

"What girl? His crazy ex? He told me about her. Trust me, they are not together Malik." I said trying to convince myself more than I was Malik.

"Whatever Andrea. Put your blinders on if you want to, but I heard through the gay vine that Mr. Javonte Football Star, was taken. He ain't all that to be sweating over anyway."

"I'm not sweating him Leaky, not at all. I'm not tripping. I mean if he got a girl that's on him. Cause I was gonna rock his world!" I said in my Wanda impression. I had to break the ice to hide my broken face shattered on the floor.

"You're too stupid. Oh Andrea I meant to thank you for the job. You are such a life saver girl."

"No Biggie Smalls B." I said in my New York voice.

"So are we gonna be working in the same building?" Malik asked in his manly voice. It comes and goes with this fool.

"I'll make sure to be at the studio when you're taken your pictures."

I got Malik some work with Mia's Magazine *Juicy*. I don't know what took me so long in making that connection. My girl runs a magazine and has tons of hook ups, and my boy is a print ad model, lovely combo. Well this was the first time Malik asked for my help with his modeling. Otherwise, I would have made the connection a long time ago. He usually kept his shit to himself, so I never knew what was going on until I picked up a Mag or Newspaper and seen him. A closed mouth don't get fed I guess. With a friend like me around all you have to do is say the word, and I got your back. Hence, Malik needed work, and Mia needed a model, and boom they both got what they asked for. Sometimes I wish I could clone myself. I need a friend like me for my damn self.

"Will I see you on my first day?"

"Yeah damn, what you want me to hold your hand and introduce you to your new classmates too honey?"

"Watch that sarcasm girl. I'm just happy to be working with my girl is that alright with you? Besides that ain't nobody thinking bout your nappy headed ass."

"Anyway Malik, I need your advice." I changed the subject faster than a tennis ball hit by Serena. I was sensitive about my nappy hair damn it.

"What's up Drea, give it to me." He said has he motioned me to sit down on the floor next to him.

"Do you think I should hide my good shit before my sister gets here?" I felt so wrong even thinking it, but damn play me once your bad, play me twice I'ma whoop your ass.

"You know your wrong right? That girl is your sister Andrea. If she says she is clean then trust her until she gives you a reason not too. But if Trina is really trying to clean up her act, than it's your job as her sister to have her back. Leave the judging for folks in the streets."

He had a point. I just didn't want to get played again.

"You remember everything she took from me before don't you? She cleaned me out. Took all my good hair. I'm hiding my good hair this time I don't care how wrong you think I am."

"It's a new day for your sister Drea, so treat it that way. Until she proves you wrong. If you treat her like a crack head then she's gonna feel like one, and may even go back to what she knows. Why try to change if the people around you still treat you like the old person your trying to get away from?"

Malik spoke from experience. He wasn't the one using, his father was. That's why they moved away during High School. When they came back, his father was clean and like I said Malik became Leaky.

"Your right, but its gonna be hard for me to trust her, let alone forgive her."

Holding grudges is as easy as breathing to me. People don't change. They evolve into a different form of themselves. Sometimes for the good, sometimes for the bad, but they don't change. They learn how to hide what they've found out people don't like, or they learn to act the way people want them to. Few people live for themselves. We're all guilty of that crime.

"You really need to work on that girl. Your gonna get a nose bleed one day from looking down on us little people from your pedestal." Malik said with his back turned toward me as he got up to go into the kitchen. I don't think I'm better than anyone, I wish people would stop saying that. I'm just telling my truth that's all.

"So what are you gonna wear on your first day Leaky?"

"I was thinking about a nice suit. What do you think?"

"I guess that's a good idea, or maybe a nice button down with some jeans. That would work too. Its really laid back at *Juicy*, plus there you'll have a wardrobe I think."

"So when I'm not taking pictures, what will I be doing?"

"You'll have to talk to them about that. I'm not sure. But I told Mia you needed a part-time, or maybe a full-time job. So she should be able to find something for you to do."

"Thank you girl. Thank you so much."

Luckily Trina already had a job. Otherwise, she would probably be working at *Juicy* too. Apart of me was excited about my sister coming to live with me. I'll take Malik's advice and give her a chance. Like he said she is family, I should be her refuge not her last resort. Being so soft made me feel kinda weak, but for my blood I'll let my guard down. I know that if Trina puts her mind to it she can evolve into a wonderful young woman like me, well not exactly like me but close.

~Juicy Days Ahead~

Tamia

I feel like a weight has been lifted off of me now that Raheem is gonna be working here. My husband has been so uptight lately. Hopefully this extra help around the office will help. I pray it does. I love El more than life itself and I will do anything for him. Even if some might say it degrades me, I'll still do it. I don't want to lose him. He's a good man. My parents told me the day of my wedding that we wouldn't last, and I want to prove them wrong. From the first time they laid eyes on him, they hated him. Granted the first impression was a little awkward, being that my ass was in the air and El was behind it. But still, you would think my parents would have gotten over that by now. El has done so much for me. I look up to him. His strength and callous attitude towards things he can't change. I envy that about him.

My Father could learn a lot from him. When I was growing up my Father thought material things was all I needed. Like I didn't need him around. Even though my Mother and Father are still together, I feel I was just raised by my Mother. My Father was never around mentally. Physically he was always in the home, but not mentally. Not how I needed him to be. My Mother used to make up so many excuses when I would ask what was wrong with him. After a while I just gave up and stopped caring. That's why I look up to El so much, he is a real man. And I will do whatever

I have to do so that he stays happy.

Today was my first day back in the office since I had the baby. Everything looked so different. I could hardly contain myself when I turned the corner and seen my girl standing there. Andrea, my best friend. We grew up together. She was one of the only people besides El that really knew me.

"I hope you liked what I did to the place Mia. Your Feng Sui was all wrong."

Andrea said as she gave me a hug. Her and El had this weird obsession with Feng Sui. Personally I don't get the whole thing. So that's why it looked so different in here. That's my girl, Miss. Control freak. I wanted my office back to how I left it, but I'm not gonna tell her that.

"I love it Andrea. I feel real creative in this space now. Has El seen it yet?" I hope he hadn't. I hope when he does he tells Andrea to put things back the way I left them.

"Nope, not yet. But I'm sure he is gonna love it. So what's my job boss?"

After I took Andrea around the office and introduced her to the rest of the staff, I showed her the office. Her office. Her workload wasn't going to be that huge, but she was my girl. Plus she would kill me if I made her sit in a cubical with the rest of the staff.

"So when is Malik planning on showing up?" I said as I rearranged the plants in front of the elevators. It was the least I could reclaim after Andreas redecorating.

"Damn babe how many people did you hire?" I heard my husband say as he smacked my ass.

"Hey baby! When did you get in?" I was surprised that El was up so early after the night we had last night. When I came back from Raheems I had planned on telling El how sorry I was, but before I could even open my mouth to apologize for leaving the way I did, he grabbed me kissed me for what seemed like hours. I don't know what got into him that night, but whatever it was I'm glad about it.

"What's up Andrea? You know your boy is gonna be working here now right?"

El said totally ignoring me, but I'm not gonna read too deep into it, like most females would. That's why we are so close, cause I don't trip on him when he does little things like that. I just go to one of my friends and let it all out.

"What you mean El? Raheem is working here now? Mia why didn't you tell me this shit. I don't need to be around his clingy ass following me around like a damn lost cause."

I wish El had given me a chance to tell her first,

but he just couldn't wait to stir up a mini drama. He knew I hadn't told Andrea yet. I wanted to tell her last week, but I just couldn't get it out.

"Oh, Mia didn't tell you?" He said as he smiled at me. He knew I didn't tell her. We just talked about it last night. I hated when he called me out like that. He knew I wouldn't say anything back to him, but I wanted to so bad.

"No, she didn't." Andrea said with a rhythmic sway in her neck.

"I like what you did to the office Andrea. It fits my style perfectly." El said as he walked back into his office.

Before I could get a chance to apologize to Andrea about Raheem, the elevator opened. And there was Raheem with Malik. I remember Malik a little bit from my younger days, but we weren't as close as he and Andrea were.

"Hi you two! Welcome to *Juicy*. Come let me introduce you to my husband." I said as I rushed the two of them past Andrea before she could say a word.

When I walked into my husbands office he was at his desk, with his eyes closed humming some commercial jingle. He was so handsome, I almost forgot why I came in there. I think he could feel our presence, because he opened his eyes and just stared into space. It was like he was looking right through us. He does that sometimes, spaces out like that. So I just snapped him out of it, like I always do.

"Honey, your new hires are here. You already know Raheem. This is Malik. Andrea's friend she was telling us about. Malik this is my husband and your boss Mr. Blaque, but I'm sure he won't mind if you call him El."

"Don't speak for me Tamia." El snapped.

"Malik, nice to meet you. Tamia will be working with you today. Raheem and I have an offsite assignment. Welcome to the company. It was very nice to meet you. Raheem come with me. Mia, lock up my office please."

El rambled those words off so fast. Before I could even respond he and Raheem were gone.

"They have a really busy day ahead. Come with me Malik."

I didn't have a clue what they had planned, but I had to act like I knew something. I mean this was my business too. I don't know what has gotten into my husband, running off like that, and leaving me with everything on my first day back. There better be a good reason for his mad dash.

El

What the fuck? What the hell? What in the good name of the Lord is happening to me? I am never going to sleep again. Not a nap, not a doze, nothing that involves closing my eyes and seeing something other than reality. I do not care how large the bags under my eyes become, I don't care how heavy my eye lids get, I will never sleep again. I though the dreams were over. I thought it was because of my wife's pregnancy that those dreams began. Then they stopped once my son was born, and everything was as peachy as my Grandma's peach cobbler. Then I fall asleep on the couch and, boom! Another damn dream. Now I come to work and the mother fucker from my dreams is working for me! This has to be one of the worst jokes God has ever played on me. I had to get away. I hope Mia worked everything out. With each dream I began to feel less and less like a man. I had to do something to feel like a man again. I had to test myself.

"If I knew working for you would be like this, I would have came along time ago." Raheem said as we pulled into the parking lot of the Black Cat, a high class strip club here in Minneapolis.

"I wanted to formally welcome you to the company man, that's all."

That wasn't all, that wasn't even the half of it. I

felt outside myself as we walked into the club. There were mirrors everywhere, so there was no escaping the fact that I was there, running from a dream. It smelled like a Laundromat in the Black Cat. They had this little old lady in there with a bottle of disinfectant that sprayed everything down. At least I knew it was clean in there. The girls weren't half bad either. The last time I came in here, it was for my bachelor party and the chicks they had in here were ass ugly. They had stretch marks in places I didn't even know you could get them. On the neck and shit. I remember one chick had a hospital bracelet on, like she had just gotten released from the emergency room. It was terrible. Times sure have changed.

"We're on the clock right?" Raheem said with his eyes glued to the dancers.

"Yeah we are."

I was short with him. Not purposely, but I was just trying to think of the right time to unload my worries on Raheem. I needed to talk. Keeping this in was making me crazy. I came to the strip club to test myself. To regain my manhood back if you know what I mean. I wanted to see if I felt the same way. I wanted to see if I still had lust in my heart for half naked females. This was one test I prayed I didn't fail. We sat down at the front of the stage. Unlike most strip joints, this one wasn't as loud. Which I liked. I know this isn't the right place to have a talk with your boy, but I needed to get something off my chest. It was hard to get Raheem's attention. I don't know what I expected. He was like a kid in a candy store.

"I don't see how any man would want to pass this up." I said trying to jump start the topic.

"Who you know that would pass these beautiful ladies up? I don't know anybody in there right mind that would pass this up. Even a married man like you."

"Yeah. Me either. I don't know about all that gay shit, you know what I mean? I just don't get it, do you?"

"Not really. But whatever makes you happy, just keep that shit away from me, you know what I sayin." Raheem said with a laugh, and his fist up waiting for a dap.

"Yeah I feel you." I said, not quite knowing how to tell my boy about my dreams, without him thinking I was gay. I knew Raheem wouldn't think I was, but you never know.

"She is the sexiest woman I have ever seen. El do you see her?"

He said as he pointed to what looked like a goddess. I must admit she was fly. And Raheem was mesmerized. If I was gonna ask him what he thought about my dreams, I had to do it now.

"Yeah she is sexy. Raheem can I ask you a question?"

I felt like a child about to tell my parents about something wrong that I had did. I felt ashamed. I looked at my Stacy Adams, took a deep breath and spit it out.

"I have been having these crazy ass dreams about.."

"Would you like a dance baby?" It was the dancer Raheem was fixated on. That hoe interrupted me.

"I sure would." Raheem said as he gave me a look that said, "I'm sorry bro, but I'm not passing her up, we will talk later."

I was just about to let it out. These demons, or whatever it was, needed to be let out and I thought that maybe if I talked to my boy about it, he would give me logical explanation to what was going on. Everything happens for a reason. I know that much. Maybe it wasn't meant for me to tell anybody, maybe this is something I have to battle on my own.

"Wanna dance baby?"

"Why not." I said with no emotion in my voice. I took a shot of Vodka and followed the dancer into the private room. This room was different from the rest of the club. There were no mirrors in here, just dim lights and music. Pretty simple. I got a few dances and gained my manhood back. Those ladies moved in ways I only seen in movies. They really upgraded from the last time I was in here. I walked out of the private room feeling like a champ.

"Be sure to give me a call." I heard the stripper say to Raheem as we exited the club.

"You got a strippers number Raheem?"

"Her name is Nicki and she is a really nice girl."

Raheem was too nice. Only he would meet a stripper and leave with her number saying, "She is a really nice girl."

"I see what your doing, a stripper is guaranteed booty. You got a lot of tension built up. I feel you."

"If that's what you think El. What did you want to ask me earlier?"

"Oh I forgot. Must not have been that important."

The ride back to work was awkward. I was quite, in a deep thought zone. Raheem was going on and on, about that damn stripper. I don't see how he got a dance from her. He knew way too much about that chick. She couldn't have been doing her job. With all that talking about her goals and shit. We all know the stripper story. "I'm a dancer, I'm in school, I'm an actress, I'm saving up to pay bills off." Blah blah blah. I heard it all before. I just wish Raheem didn't fall in the trap.

But I guess that's how we differ. I know a lot about women and he believes everything they say. Major difference. I am glad we came to the club though. It was what I needed. I passed my manhood test with flying colors. I was so turned on from all those dancers, I had to keep looking down at my ring to keep me from doing something I might regret. I think I got the answer I was looking for. My wife alone just wasn't doing it for me. We needed to spice things up a bit. I guess the boredom was getting to my head, big and little, and those dreams were a product of bedroom boredom plain and simple.

Raheem

Taking this job at *Juicy* turned out to be a good move for me. Even though I have only been there for a couple of weeks, I can already see things starting to turn around for the better. This job isn't as bad as I thought it would be. I would have never imagined working with El would be so laid back. We might be boys and all, but when it comes to El and his work, he is all about getting shit done. The first day on the job, we went to The Black Cat. I thought El had lost his damn mind, taking me there on the clock. That wasn't like him at all. Luckily he was in the mood for the club, even though it seemed like he came there to get something off his chest. I don't know exactly what his problem was because right when he began to talk I saw Nicki.

She was one of the dancers there, the finest dancer there. Her body was banging. From head to toe, she was hot like fire. She has flawless brown skin, sexy brown eyes and did I mention a crazy body. It's like she was made to dance. I couldn't keep my eyes off of her. And when she asked me if I wanted a dance, I had to leave my boy in the middle of our conversation. Whatever he had on his mind must not have been that important because when I asked him what was up he acted like it was nothing. I have known El for way too long, and I know when something wasn't right with him. I could tell he had something on his mind from the moment I walked in his office. He looked like he had seen a ghost. I'm not the one to try to pry something out of someone, especially a grown ass man, but I can tell something is up. He walks around the office with his head watching his feet, as if he's counting his steps. Maybe that's how he works, I don't know. It just doesn't seem like El at all. Other than that everything else is going good. Besides running into Andrea every once and a while I'm staying focused on the job. Even though that girl dogged me, I still love her like nothing happened. I'm trying to keep my mind off of her, but every time I see her I fall deeper and deeper. It's hard enough trying to get over someone when their not around, but it's even harder when you have to see that person every day at your job. I think she has been dressing just to mess with my head, because she has been looking extra sexy. Her skirts have been just short enough, and shirts tight enough. Getting over this girl wouldn't be so bad if she didn't look so damn good.

"You look bored. Sorry if I kept you waiting too long." Nicki said as she slid into the booth at Red Lobster.

I had invited her out with me this weekend. We have talked almost every day since we met at the club. She seems real cool, but with women out here these days you never know.

"I'm not bored, just anxious for your arrival

that's all. So how was your week Nicki?"

I couldn't think of anything else to say. I knew how her week was, I talked to her damn near every day. It's just that on the phone words come a lot easier for me than in person. Especially since she is so fine, it's hard to focus.

"Busy. Just working and going to class. Other than that nothing much is going on."

Nicki is studying at the University, majoring in business. She is putting her self through school. I admire that about her, cause school is expensive and without any outside help you are bound to go broke. But she seems like she has her head on her shoulders, cause she's never without dough.

"So Raheem how are you doing today?" She asked as she held my hand from across the table.

"I'm doing a lot better now that you're here."

I couldn't help but smile. It's been a real long time since I had been out with someone like Nicki. She is more than just physically beautiful, but she has a personality that I'm not used to and I couldn't wait to get to know better.

"Even though it has only been a couple of weeks since we have known each other, I'm really feeling you. I hope that doesn't sound crazy of me, but that is just how I feel. You're not like most men I know. Once they find out where I work they feel I'm easy and try to get in my pants before trying to get to know me, but not you. You haven't even tried to take me to your place."

"I'm not like most men. There is more to you than sex appeal. I saw that from our first conversation. Plus you know I stay with my Mom, and bringing you home wouldn't feel right."

Nicki knew I was living my Mother and it didn't seem to phase her at all. I told her about my job, and what was going on. She knew I was creeping on the come up.

"I have known men older than you, without the goals you have, and they still try to bring me back to their Mom's house. From what I've seen men don't care too much about where they get it, just as long as they get it."

"Oh well I'm nothing like that. There is more to women then just sex. When it comes I'll receive it, but I'm not gonna force it." I said telling a half truth.

The reason I'm not gonna force sex, is because I'm afraid I forget how to do it all together. Flirting is easy, it's the foreplay and the sex that I might be a little rusty at.

"We should catch a movie after lunch, there is this new one out that I have been dying to see." Nicki said with her face buried in the menu.

But before I could agree with her on prolonging our time together our waitress interrupted us.

"Trina? Is that you?" I said to this woman that looked just like Andrea's sister, but was much cleaner.

"Hey Raheem! I didn't even notice you. You're looking good. How have you been?"

"I have been doing good, real good. You look great Trina."

I couldn't believe how much she had cleaned up. Trina used to be the shit back in the day. Then she got hooked on drugs. It was so sad. I can remember Andrea telling me about all the hurt her and her family was going through. I loved Trina like family, and I was hurt when I heard about her drug habit. I'm just glad to see that she has cleaned up her act. She was looking real good.

"Thank you Raheem. So what can I get for you two?" She said as she looked over at Nicki who was still behind the menu.

"Oh I'm sorry let me introduce you two. Trina this is my friend Nicki, and Nicki this is Trina. We grew up together."

When Nicki finally came from behind the menu that was shielding her to greet Trina, a devilish smile came across her face.

"Trina right? Nice to meet you." Nicki said as she stretched her hand out.

"Raheem how long have you known her?" Trina asked as she ignored Nicki's hand. She spoke as if she didn't know me and her sister weren't together anymore.

"Long enough." Nicki answered for me. I don't know what was going on, but I heard a little too much attitude coming from the both of them.

"Do you two ladies know each other?" I asked.

"Not at all. I have never seen her in my life." Nicki calmly answered.

"I'll be back with some water for you two." Trina said as she rushed to the back.

"What was that all about? How do you know her? She was acting like you used to be her man back in the day or something." Nicki said with her eyes focused on mine.

"I used to date her sister, I'm not sure if she was filled in on the news that we are no longer together."

"Well when she comes back maybe you should fill her in." Nicki demanded.

"This isn't the place for all that Nicki, but I'm

sure she will find out for herself soon enough."

"Well if you won't tell her I'm your new woman then I will."

"My woman? Nicki I just met you." I knew she was too good to be true.

"Not like that, I just mean she *is* serving us and I don't want no special sauce in my special sauce if you know what I mean. Just let her know your seeing other people now, so she won't think your dogging her sister."

"If it will make you more comfortable Nicki." I said with hesitation in my voice. I just didn't feel like this was the right place to bring it up, and I didn't even know if that was what Trina's problem was. After all, her attitude was directed at Nicki, not me.

"Here are your waters, are you ready to order?" The waiter said.

"What happened to our waitress?" Nicki asked.

"She went home sick. I will be serving you today."

I don't know what was wrong with Trina. She was acting really weird, and I can't believe she just left like that. What was the rush? Nicki and I spent the whole time at the Red Lobster talking about Andrea. She had so many questions, which isn't uncommon for the new woman in your life to want to know about the past woman. The more I talked about how Andrea treated me, the more my feelings began to change towards Andrea. I hope Nicki will be the one to help me get over that speed bump in my road called Andrea. The way she took interest in my past, made me feel that she might be the push I need to move on.

Tamia

I love my husband to death, but I don't know how much more I can take. I thought that once we got some extra help around the office he would be less stressed out, but it seems like the total opposite has happened. First he and Raheem have some secret offsite meeting, and then when I ask about it he curses me out. Telling me I need to mind my business, and to focus something else. Whatever that is suppose to mean. Second he has been really distant at work, daydreaming more than usual. And when I snap him out of it, he looks as if he was caught doing something wrong. Then he starts to treat me like a queen, kissing me and telling me how much I mean to him. Then in that same day we can be at home, and he will totally ignore me, unless he is ordering me to fix him dinner or to change the channel for him. At first I thought he was just going through his little attitude changes that he usually does, but they don't last for this long. He snaps out of it within a day or so, but this has lasted a couple of weeks. After council from Andrea I have decided to talk to him. I'm not sure what I want to say, or how I want to say it, but I do know that I need to have a talk with my husband.

"What did you want Mia?" El asked as he plopped down on the couch. I had told him last night I needed to talk to him, and he waited until tonight to acknowledge my request.

"We need to talk baby." I said not knowing how to start the ball rolling.

"Obviously Tamia. So what's on your mind baby girl?" He said has he pulled me closer to him on the couch.

"What's been up with you lately El? You have been acting so unlike yourself. You daydream all the time, your extra sweet to me at work but when we get home you act as if I don't exist. What's going on with you? I thought maybe the extra help would make things better, but I feel like they are worse."

There I said it. Not everything, but the most important things. Well most of the important things.

"What do you want from me Mia? I'm stressed out. I'm sorry I do run a company, and sometimes when a lot of shit is going on, I will on occasion get a little stressed. I'm sorry if that doesn't fit into the neatly packed perfect life you have in your mind. But this is what happens honey, sometimes a man can get a little tight."

I could hear the sarcasm in his voice. When he acts like this, I feel like he isn't even listening to me. Like he doesn't hear me saying that I want to make it all better. I don't want to start an argument with him, but I have to get to the bottom of what it is that's bothering him. All I want is for him to be happy, because when he's happy I'm happy. And right now

I'm not too happy.

"I know the job can be a little hard at times El, but.."

"Tamia. Baby listen. I'm sorry if you feel like I have been ignoring you. Yes this job is hard at times, and yes I am stressed out right now, but I don't have any right to take that out on you. I'm sorry." El said as he pulled me closer for a hug.

It felt good to hug my husband, I had barely touched him this past week, so this hug was feeling real good. Like everything was okay. He apologized, I think he knows how I feel now.

"Its fine El, I just want us to be okay. When you get stressed, I get stressed, and I just want you to get back to your old self again. That's all."

That wasn't all. I wanted him to treat me like his equal while at work, and ask me to do things, instead of ordering me around like I was some damn maid. I wanted him to help me when the baby wakes up in the middle of the night, I wanted him to talk to me about what was going on with him, like he used to when we first got together. I wanted him to fix me dinner some nights, and wash clothes and clean the house sometimes. With the lack of attention I have been getting lately, I wouldn't mind for the return of the dreaded head schedule.

"Mia, you know what I think we need?"

Please say a vacation to an island. Like the one where Jay-Z took Beyonce. Somewhere romantic where we can dine out every night, and dine in every morning. Somewhere where the water is so blue, you can see all the way to the bottom. Or please say we need a nanny to help us around the house. So I wouldn't have to spend all my time in the baby's room and in the kitchen, then back to the baby's room.

"No what?" I said secretly crossing my fingers behind my back.

"You promise you won't get mad?" El said as he sat up like an eager child.

"Yes baby I promise I won't get mad just tell me what you think we need."

Whatever it was, I know it wasn't bad because he was smiling from ear to ear.

"Ok. I was thinking about what we could do to liven things up a bit, something to get our juices flowing.

"What baby! What is it?"

I was so excited. I have a feeling its gonna be a vacation. Finally!

"A threesome." He said as he looked at me with his bedroom eyes.

"Oh." I said trying to keep an open mind to my husband's thoughts, but damn. A threesome. Are you serious? I have never even looked at a female like that, let alone thought about what a threesome would be like. It didn't seem right to me.

"Oh? What's that mean?"

"I mean, I never really thought about anything like that. What made you think of that?"

"Nothing really it just came to me."

"You mean me, you and another woman?"

"Yeah, I damn sure didn't mean you, me and no other man." He snapped.

"That's not what I meant El, I'm just saying I don't feel totally comfortable sharing you with another woman."

"It's not like that at all, there are different ways you can have a threesome Tamia." El said.

He spoke as if he was the professor of How To Have a Threesome 101. I love my husband more than life, but I don't know about this.

"I know the ways El, I just don't know if that's really what we need right now."

"Ok Mia, if that's how you feel. Just remember you asked me what you could do to make me happy, and I just told you. Take that information and do with it what you want."

"El please, don't act like your happiness is all on me. I have been trying not to argue with you since you have been in such a funky mood but.."

"But what baby?" He said as he kissed my hand, then my shoulder, then my neck, damnit! I hate it when he did that. Now I forgot what I was complaining about.

"Nothing, but nothing baby." I said as I enjoyed my attention I was finally getting.

"Good. You know what I want you to do?" He said as the kisses became more sensual.

"What's that El?"

"Just think about what I said, I know it's a lot to just throw at you. So just take sometime to think about it. For me?"

"Okay I'll think about it El."

"Thank you baby. That's why I love you so much, you're so open minded. How about tonight I take care of dinner? How would you like that?"

"I would love it!" I said too excited for my own good. I can't believe El was finally gonna cook for me. Since I had the baby, I have been the one cooking and cleaning. A home cooked meal was sounding real good, especially if I didn't have to cook it.

"Good. I'm gonna go pick up some KFC. I have been craving that damn chicken for days. I'll take Laurence with me so you can have some alone time while were gone."

What the hell? KFC? Are you serious? He calls that taking care of dinner? And the only thing he means by "alone time" is time to clean up while he's gone.

"Thanks baby." I said as I got up and gave him a kiss.

"I might make a couple of stops, so you'll have about two hours or so." He said as he picked up Laurence.

"Drive safe honey it's really slippery out!" I yelled as he put the baby in his car seat and drove off.

"Where's the phone?" I said aloud to myself. I had to call Andrea.

Andrea

"What's wrong with you?" I yelled at myself as I ripped pages out from my journal. I hated when I felt like a dumb little girl in love. Then like a dummy I document it, so I can read just how stupid I was at a later date. I was writing about Raheem. Of all the people, places and the things in the world, I was writing about Raheem. I can't stop thinking about him or dreaming about him, and now that he works with me I can't stop writing about him. This is so unlike me, to be stressing over a man. Please, not me. I got too much going for me right now, shit he should be stressing over me. Which he is. I can see the love still in his eyes for me. He thinks I don't feel his eyes on me when I pass him, but I do. He still wants me, and he always will. I'm glad he has a good job now, pretty soon the car and the house will come to follow, and then we can get back together.

Even though I want to be with him now, I can't. He has to know that I was serious when I told him he needed to man up. I know he got this job for me, a way to get me back, and it's working. But until I see the fruits of his labor, he can continue to lust over me. Once I found out Raheem was going to be working at *Juicy,* I had to get some sexier clothes, quick, fast and in a hurry. I have to keep his attention, even if we're not together. I should charge Mia's ass for my new wardrobe. She didn't even prepare me for Raheem.

When I saw him, I thought I was dreaming. There was no way that my ex and I could be working at the same place. Mia has been so damn worried about pleasing El that she forgot about the most important thing. Pleasing me.

"I was just thinking about you Mia." I said while closing my journal. I felt like a 10 year old, keeping a damn journal.

"Really? Girl I need to talk to you."

"Yeah I need to talk to you too. Now that were not at work, tell me what the hell was up with Raheem being at *Juicy*?"

"Nothing really, El just felt we needed some help around the office, so we decided to hire Raheem. Sorry I didn't tell you sooner, I just haven't been thinking straight lately."

"Its aight girl, I was just shocked that's all, but you know what.."

"Drea I really need to talk to you." She snapped. It must have been important cause she just cut me off mid sentence.

"I'm sorry girl, what's up?"

"Remember I was telling you how El was acting kinda distant lately. Like he has just been ignoring me. So after I talked to you, I finally sat down and had a talk with him."

"Good, you need to tell that man how you feel. Just be real."

"Anyway, so we talked, he held me close as I shared my concerns with him." Mia said in her office voice. I couldn't stand when she dragged around the issue.

"Mia damn, just tell me what the problem is."

"Well I asked him what I could do to make him happier, to bring the joy back into his eyes. Cause lately he has been so out of it. Like the other day.."

I had to cut her off. I think I have the shortest attention span known to man, because I hated too much detail. Shit just get to the point.

"Mia what is it!" I yelled.

"He told me he wants to have a threesome."

"What? Get the hell outta here. A threesome? What did you say?"

I know what she said, she probably said, "Well okay baby only if I can pick the girl," or "I don't know, but if you really want to then I guess so." She would do anything for that man, but if I had anything to do with it, she wouldn't be doing that.

"At first I was like I don't think so, but then he

told me to think about. So I'm thinking about it. Andrea I don't know what to do. What would you do?"

"First of all it wouldn't be me, okay? I wish my man would ask me to have a damn threesome, like I'm not all he needs. Not that I have a man, but you know what I mean."

"You think it's because of me?"

"No, that's not what I mean."

"Well what do you think I should do?"

I hated when Mia acted like I had the answer to everything, I mean I do know a lot and my advice is golden at times, but damn. It's like she wears a WWAD bracelet, and every time something goes down she looks at it and thinks, What Would Andrea Do?

"Maybe he just wants to spice things up. Have you tried toys or movies?"

"Toys? Yes. Movies? Yes. I don't know what's left."

"A home movie?"

I never understood why Mia came to me with her sex questions, being that I'm a virgin I'm not the best resource when it comes to this topic.

"When we first got married, he had mentioned something about that. He said it was always a fantasy of his. I like that idea better than a threesome."

"I might not have had sex before, but I do know that it can't be a good thing to bring a stranger in your bed. Can you imagine another woman kissing, and touching on you and your husband? And do you think after you all have tried it, he won't want to do that shit again? He is a man, ass is ass, and two is a whole lot better than one. Especially if his own wife said the shit is okay."

"Your right Drea, but I have to do something to bring that spark back. I'm gonna try the home movie idea. Now I just have to find a good time to tell him."

"Wait until he has that whole threesome thing out of his head, then when he least expects it, drop that bomb girl."

"So enough about me and my dilemmas. How is Trina doing?"

"Even though it's only been a couple of weeks, things are going really good. I haven't talked to her as much as she talked to me. She keeps going on and on about how proud I'm gonna be of her and shit like that."

"I'm so glad she is getting better. Are you charging her to stay with you?"

"Hell yeah. This ain't no free ride. You want to get prepared for the real world, well let's start with rule #1, paying bills. You know what's funny is that when she moved in, I sat her down and laid out the bills, and all the expenses and she paid me two months up front."

"She must be doing real good then if she's throwing out money like that." Mia said.

"Andrea are you home?" I heard my sister yell. What the hell was she doing home so early, I thought she had to work til close tonight? I swear she better not have gotten fired already.

"Mia, I'll see you at work on Monday I got to go." I threw the phone on my bed and went into the living room, where Trina was waiting for me. Whatever she had to say, it didn't look like it was good news.

"What's wrong? Is everything alright? Is it your job?"

"Andrea sit down so we can talk." Trina said as she looked me dead in the eyes. She better not tell me some bull about quitting her job or even about her picking up her habit. I shouldn't have got so excited just because she dropped some dough down. I thought everything was cool, but by the look in her eyes, I could tell it wasn't.

El

"How did you want your burger done Mia?" I yelled across the backyard to my wife.

"Medium I guess, but not red." She answered back.

We were having a barbeque and I was the designated chef for the day. I'm okay with cooking for a lot of people. For the last couple of months I have been cooking and catering to my wife. Mostly out of guilt for what I asked of her. In my head the whole threesome idea sounded real cool. But once I heard myself ask my wife to have one, it didn't sound as good. I haven't brought it back up since that night. I don't even know how we would do the whole thing anyway. The only female friend of Mia's that I would even consider would be Andrea, and that idea is wrong on too many levels. My thoughts have been so out of wack lately. I have been so preoccupied with trying to keep that man out of my head, I ended up letting a bunch of bullshit take his place.

That's why I decided to have this barbeque with my friends. I just want to relax and enjoy my company, but mostly catch up with my boy Raheem. You would think that with us working at the same company that we talk all the time, but we don't. I mean, he talks about his girl, and how much he digs her, and all that mushy bullshit. Then when he finally gets done talking about that damn girl and I try to get a word in, she calls and he runs. But besides the new meat in his life, I'm proud of my boy. He has been working his ass off. He's making major figures now. He's moving on up real fast.

"What up boy!" I said as I gave Raheem a hand shake on his free hand, the other one was holding Nicki's hand. Clingy ass female.

"Chillin man that's all. El this is Nicki. I'm glad I get to finally introduce you two." Raheem said.

"It seems like I already know you, as much as Raheem talks about you El." Nicki said as she gave me a hug.

I wonder if Raheem felt weird since I had already seen Nicki's goodies when we were at the strip club. Personally that would fuck with me, but I guess he's just happy to have someone to keep his mind off Andrea.

"Yeah me too. Nice to finally put a face to the name I hear so often." I said.

I had already put the body to the name, but I forgot what her face looked like. Oops.

"Raheem I left something in the car, can you come help me get it?" Nicki said like she was a damn five year old. Get it your damn self, me and my boy had some catching up to do, plus I needed some help with all this food my wife bought for me to cook.

"Yeah, I'll be right back El." Raheem said as he skipped off with that damn girl and left me with all this meat to cook by myself.

"You need some help?" Malik asked as he walked up to the grill.

I have been trying my best to ignore his ass, but Andrea invited him to the barbeque. Malik is probably an alright guy. I just don't want to run the risk of those dreams returning. But the guy did work for me, I guess the least I could do was to be hospitable.

"Yeah, thanks."

"You don't remember me do you?" Malik asked as he flipped the burgers on the back grill.

"From where?" Where the hell would I remember him from. We had already established the fact that he used to work at that corner store near my house. Where else would I know him from?

"Do you remember Brenda?"

"From Middle School? Big booty Brenda? Hell yeah I remember her. Why is that your family or something? Cause you know we used to date right? I think I was that girls first." I said, wishing I had kept that last part out, but oh well as long as she wasn't his kin.

"Naw you weren't that girls first." Malik said while he laughed.

"How you know?"

"Cause I was. I can't believe you don't remember me El, Malik Hatcher from Franklin Middle School." Malik said.

Oh shit! Hatcher the panty snatcher! You have got to be kidding me. This fool was a little freak.

"What? So your Hatcher the panty snatcher huh? Man you stole my girl!"

I couldn't believe that was this Malik. This was the guy I thought was gay? Now I really had nothing to worry about. He was a nasty little negro back in the day. He had all the fly girls.

"When I found out that LL was gonna be my boss, I couldn't stop laughing. I knew you wouldn't recognize me, but once I told you my last name, it would all come back to you." Malik said.

They used to call me LL back in the day, cause the ladies loved me, and still do. Malik was a cool cat. We talked and drank while we grilled the food. From the sounds of things, he seemed straighter than they come, even though he didn't really talk to much about chicks. Mostly sports and shit like that, so that was cool too. I feel kind of stupid for ignoring him this whole time because of those damn dreams.

"What up Leak!" Andrea yelled as she ran up to the grill with some bodybuilder looking cat.

"What's good Andrea? You don't see anyone else?" I said.

"El I see you. Damn give me a chance. How are yall doing today?" She asked liked she really cared.

I knew the only thing she really cared about was where Raheem was, so she could show of her new man.

"Aight. Who's your friend?" I said as I looked her boy toy up and down. I'm used to seeing her with Raheem. It feels kinda weird to see both of them with someone besides each other. Besides this fool looked like he was trying way too hard. I love Andrea like family, so whoever this cat was, he had better act right.

"Malik, El this is Javonte. Javonte these are my two friends Malik and El." Andrea said like she was showing off a prized pooch.

"Javonte?" Malik said questioning Andrea.

"Yeah Javonte, well I'm gonna go find Mia. See yall." Andrea said as she rushed off.

"You know him?" I asked Malik.

"I don't know him, but I know of him. I didn't even know they were talking." Malik said.

Andrea is my girl and all, but she is so see through. She brings this fool to my barbeque knowing that Raheem is gonna be here with his arm candy. If her own friend didn't know about Javonte, it must not be that serious. I just hope it doesn't turn into the Maury show once these four come into contact.

Raheem

"I just don't understand why we had to come all the way back to my place, just to get this potato salad. We could have picked some up from the grocery store."

"Cause I made it Raheem. I don't want to bring store bought potato salad to your friends house. I wanted to make a good first impression." Nicki said as she hopped out my truck and walked back into the barbeque.

It was kind of late for her to be worried about first impressions. I mean she met me and my boy at the strip club. He had already seen her butt ass naked I'm sure he could careless about where the potato salad came from. When I first met Nicki, I didn't think her job would be an issue, but now that we have gotten some what serious, I have changed my views. At first it was kind of flattering to know that other men were lusting over what I had, but that gets old fast. I thought real long and hard about how to bring this up to Nicki. She is a sweet girl, but when she gets upset things can get a little out of control. After about a week or two of planning out how I was going to bring it up to her, I finally decided to just do it. I had cooked her favorite meal. Crab legs, mashed potatoes, broccoli and her favorite type of cheesecake for desert. I lit all the candles I had and spread them all over my town home. I brought her two dozen roses and when I went to pick her up I surprised her with them in front of all her co workers. She was so happy when she saw me, I just knew that when I told her how I felt about her dancing she would agree with me and consider quitting. I can be so naive at times.

"Nigga when you met me I was dancing, what in the hell makes you think that just because you caught feelings that I'm gonna stop. This is my job for now Raheem, and unless your going to pay my bills and take care of me, you ain't got a damn thing to say to me about when and how I make my money." She said while she blew out most of the candles. "You think you can buy me some damn flowers, cook me a meal and light a couple of candles, you think that's gonna change my mind? Fuck your flowers Raheem! Fuck your food, and fuck your little mood you were trying to set! I'm sick of men trying to change me, I am who I am. Love it or leave it!"

By the time she was done cussing me out, the roses I bought for her, were torn up all over the house, the food was thrown on the floor and half my dishes were broken along side of them. When she started going off, I was in shock, I had never seen a female spazz out like that before. I had to make sure my next move, was my best move before she turned her anger toward more than just my dishes.

"Nicki calm down, it's not that serious. You

ain't gotta be breaking my shit like this, all I did was tell you how I felt, that's all. If you don't agree then just say so, but don't throw a fit like a child."

"A child? Who you calling a child? You punk ass nigga! Just cause you got some income coming in, and got you a house and a ride, you think you're better than me now is that it? Cause you wasn't talking this shit when you were at home with your Momma. You think you grown cause you got some bills now?"

"My money ain't got nothing to do with the way I feel about your dancing at that club Nicki, don't try to turn it around on me. I thought I could tell you how I felt and we could discuss it like adults, but I guess I was wrong. Clean up the mess you made and get the hell out of my house." I really didn't have time for that petty bullshit.

"I'm not your maid!"

"And you're not my child either. I'm not gonna clean up after your grown ass Nicki!" I yelled.

I hated to yell, but by the way she was acting I didn't know what she was going to do next. She looked at me like I had lost my mind when I handed her the broom. To my surprise she took the broom and started to clean up. I didn't want to stand there and watch her, so I went up stairs to smoke a black. She had me a little stressed. When she was done, she came up stairs and knocked on my bedroom door.

"Raheem I'm sorry. I really am." She said with tears in her eyes. I didn't know if they were sincere tears, or if she was just embarrassed about how she had acted.

"Nicki I like you a lot, but if we can't even have a simple discussion, then I don't see the point of us trying to move on."

"I'm sorry I don't know what has gotten into me Raheem. I understand your point I really do, it's just that I make really good money right now. Every man that I have been with always tries to change me, and I'm sick of that."

"I'm not trying to change you Nicki. I'm just letting you know how I feel. That's all. I didn't say I wasn't gonna be with you if you didn't stop, we didn't even get that far in the conversation. I'm just saying it makes me uncomfortable when I know other men are looking at you like that, that's all."

"I'll stop soon Raheem I promise."

Her promise went in one ear and out the other. After that little scene she made I started to have second thoughts about Nicki. I haven't brought it up since that day, and I don't plan on it. I'm just gonna take it day by day with her. I just don't know how much longer I can take her job and not to mention her crazy ass temper.

"Where should I set this?" Nicki asked Mia.

"Come with me, we can put it in the kitchen." Mia said looking at me like I had done something wrong. She didn't like me with any female other than Andrea, and by the look she gave Nicki she wasn't too happy with my choice.

The way the men were looking at Nicki, I could tell they had been to the Black Cat a time or two. Either that or they were just admiring her shape. She was looking good. She had on gold strapped heals, tight blue jeans with a gold and red Baby Phat shirt that fit her perfectly. Her hair was back in a long pony tail and she had on those around the way girl hoop earrings. She looked like she had stepped right out of a King Magazine, which was a good and a bad thing at the same time.

"Where's Andrea?" Nicki eagerly asked.

"Why are you so pressed on meeting her?" I snapped.

Every five minutes she was asking me about Andrea. What does she look like? Is she skinny? Is she cute? It was starting to get on my nerves.

"Is that her with that man?" Nicki happily pointed her out. "Come on lets go say hi." She said pulling on my like a an excited child.

"Yeah that's her." I said trying to act as if Andrea with another man didn't faze me.

The truth is, it did. She moves on so fast. It's hard to believe she just got out of a relationship a couple of months ago. I guess you can't sit around forever, I didn't. Physically I didn't I had a lot of stress built up, but emotionally a part of me is still waiting around, holding on to the dream of her. Seeing her with someone else makes me realize it's time to wake up.

Andrea

I had to bust a move before Malik busted me out. I don't know what he would have said, but I know it wouldn't have been nice. He is probably tight because I didn't tell him Javonte was back in the picture, but oh well he'll get over it. Javonte called me out of the blue a couple of weeks ago. He told me some long drawn out story about a family emergency and he had to leave the state for a couple of months. Which would have been a good excuse if I wouldn't have seen him a month before.

Usually I would have cursed his lying ass out, but I was a little lonely so I over looked it. Plus I had just heard that Raheem had a new chick in his life, and two can play at that game. When Trina came home that day early from work, I didn't know what to think. Thank God she was just trying to tell me about Raheem and his so-called girl. She didn't know we weren't together, and thought that he was cheating on me, which is too funny. Raheem would be a fool to cheat on me. When she was telling about his new chick, she seemed like she was holding something back, like there was more to the story, and I was starting to think it was by the way she was acting. Trina was so focused on trying to figure out how we broke up and trying to get us back together, I started to think that Raheem had said something to her. I still think there was more to what she told me, I can tell when my sister is hiding something from me, I just couldn't dream of what it would be that involved me and Raheem. Because even if she didn't know we weren't together, it wasn't that serious for her to rush home from work, just to tell me that. I mean it was serious, but not that serious. Raheem with a new chick doesn't scare me. He will always be mine. If he wants to play his self into thinking that he is over me, then he can go ahead and do that, but when I look into his eyes and our past together I see the truth.

"Is that your ex?" Javonte asked looking over at Malik.

"Who Malik? No that's one of my best friends. He was just surprised I hadn't told him about you yet."

"I'm not special enough for you to tell your closest friends about me?" Javonte said.

For Javonte to be a manly football playing man, he sure acts like a damn female sometimes. He is sexy and all, but damn I get sick of answering his insecure questions.

"Of course you are Jay, I just haven't had time to talk to him lately that's all." Damn!

"Andrea?"

I heard Raheem say from behind me as he tapped my shoulder. He probably wants to talk. He probably saw me and Javonte walk in here hand in hand, and he got a little jealous. Now he wants to talk and work things out. Things never change. I couldn't wait to turn around and see what he had to say.

"Hey, this is Nicki she wanted to meet you." Raheem said trying not to make eye contact with me.

For real? I could give a good hot damn about who that hoe was, all I knew is she wasn't me. She wasn't even all that cute. In a split second I checked that hoe out from head to toe. Her shoes where from the beauty supply store, her ponytail was too, and it was three shades off of her real hair color. She was about four months past due of and in desperate need of a relaxer, her jeans were so tight her feet were turning blue, and her so called Baby Phat shirt, had the spelling all wrong. It said Baby Fat! She was doing way too much, but not doing enough. It was kind of sad.

"What's up Nicki, I'm Andrea as you already know. Raheem, Nicki, this is Javonte."

"What's good man?" Raheem said to Javonte as they shook hands.

"Nice to meet you both." Javonte said as pulled me close into him. This just didn't feel right.

"Raheem can I speak with you for a second?" I said.

"I'll be right back Nicki."

I could careless about the dirty look she gave me, she didn't know it yet but Raheem was just using her to make me jealous. And I'm sorry to say, it was working. I'll be damned if I'm gonna let Raheem go and be with some other chick. He is what he is because of me and no chick from the block is gonna come in and enjoy what I had built from the ground up.

"What is it Andrea?" Raheem said as he closed the patio door behind him.

He was looking so good. He had on a button down, with cuff links that wouldn't stop shining. His jeans were pressed just right. He was wearing fresh Tims that looked like they just came straight out the box. He was so sexy.

"Your funny Raheem, you know that? You gonna bring that hood rat to our friends home, just to make me jealous."

"Andrea, everything I do doesn't involve a thought of you. Not anymore."

"So what are you saying Raheem? You don't care about how I feel now?"

"What's your problem, you broke up with me remember? You told me I needed to grow up and be a man. It's not my fault that instead of you staying with me, you decided to leave. You did that Andrea, not me. Now I have a good job, a car and a home of my own, and now you want to try to work it out?"

"Who said anything about working it out Raheem?"

At least no out loud. In my head I did want to work it out, but my pride wouldn't let me tell him that.

"What was your purpose for tearing me away from my girlfriend and bringing me in here Andrea?"

"Your girlfriend? That doesn't even sound right."

"It might not to you, but its music to my ears. Listen, I have a girl and by the looks of it you have a man. So either we can move on and be friends, or we can just move on."

It's like the roles of our relationship had reversed. He had really moved on, and I'm starting to think that no matter what I say or do nothing is going to change his mind, or his heart.

"Do you still love me?"

"Of course I do Andrea, but I'm sick of your games, and the way you left me was wrong. I thought you had my back, but when it got a little rough for me you left me. I'm not gonna lie and say I'm over you, but I'm trying to get there. I gotta go out there with

Nicki before she gets upset."

"What about me being upset, you just gonna walk out in the middle of our conversation?"

"Your happiness is Javonte's responsibility now, not mine." Raheem said as he walked away from me and into the arms of that trick.

I didn't want to believe it, but it was right in my face, Raheem had found someone else and it had nothing to do with me. When he walked away from me, I felt like the biggest ass in the world. He was right, I was wrong to leave him like that, but that's how he learns. That's why he has a job, and all that other shit, because I left him and he knew that he needed to change things. If I hadn't walked away from him, he would still be at his mother's house and catching the bus to the unemployment office. I made him a success, and this is the thanks I get?

"Sorry about that Jay." I said as I kissed him on the cheek.

"What was that all about?"

"Work. Just talking about work. Someone is about to get fired, I just wanted to give him a heads up that's all."

"He getting fired?"

"No, but someone close to him won't be around

much longer. But enough about that, let's eat."

I decided to let my guard down, and let Javonte in. The more we talked, the more I realized how much of a nice person he was. He was just my type, but I was too blind to see it before. I was so busy trying to make Raheem jealous that I hadn't even gave him a chance, until now. He was funny, kind and had a Colgate smile like crazy. He is sexy as hell, now that I think about it. For the rest of the day at the barbeque all we did was talk, and the more we talked, the more I realized, it was time to move on. I just hope my heart would follow.

El

"I'm glad we got rid of Randy Moss, with his cocky ass." I said as I knocked back my fourth beer.

"Your crazy El, Randy was the team, now what we got? A bunch of rookies and a quarterback? Please, I think I'm a Raiders fan now!" Malik said.

I have been hanging with Malik for the past couple of months, and not just because Raheem has been too busy with his head stuck up Nicki's ass. But Malik is a cool cat. He's a real deep dude, has a lot of insight on real life issues. It seems like he has a story for every issue I have, like he has been through it all. But I know one story he hasn't been through. I vowed that I wouldn't tell anyone about my dreams, and I especially shouldn't tell the person the dreams were about, but something was telling me to just let it out while I finally had the courage, liquid courage.

"Hey Malik, remember when you were telling me how you thought something was wrong with me when you first met me." I said as I knocked back my fifth and final beer.

"Yeah, when you used to come into that corner store I used to work at. I thought you had a mental problem for real, but I didn't even recognize that it was you, until you brought it up to me at work."

"You wanna hear something funny?" I asked

hoping I wasn't about to mess up my new found friendship.

"Hit me." Malik said.

"I was having these dreams. Weird type dreams and you were in them. Before I even officially met you."

"What type of dreams? Was I chasing you or what? I'm good at analyzing dreams."

"Don't think I'm funny or nothing like that, but you were trying to seduce me, like on some gay shit. It was messed up. That's why when I would see you I would mash out. It just didn't feel right. But now that I've gotten to know you, I'm glad I can finally get this off my chest. You don't seem like that kind of guy so it's all good. I haven't told anyone besides you."

I felt a little weird telling him that, but like I said without those beers, I highly doubt those words would have ever escaped my lips.

"What kind of guy do I seem like?" Malik asked. It was like he didn't even hear what I said about the dreams, but hey if he wanted to act like he didn't hear it, then I'll act like I didn't said it.

"I mean you're not gay, and now that we are cool, I'm just glad I could get that out my system."

"Get what out your system?"

He was asking me these questions like he was trying to psychoanalyze me.

"Get that dream and those thoughts out my system, shit I don't know. I'm just glad I could let it out."

"What if I told you I was gay. What would you do then?"

"What are you trying to say?" I said as I focused my eyes on his. I had officially lost my buzz.

"I am gay El." Malik said.

This has to be another one of those damn dreams. I sat there for a couple of minutes in silence, waiting for something to disappear like it did last time. Nothing happened. So the gay ass dreams I was having, were about me and a gay ass man, that I didn't even know was gay! What the hell was going on? I just had to open my big mouth and say something, now he's gonna think I want him or some gay shit like that.

"Your bullshitting me right? Are you trying to be funny? I tell you about my gay dreams and you tell me you're a gay. You play too much man for real."

"I'm not *a* gay, I *am* gay."

I had to take another minute. I had to say my next comment in my head to myself first, then if it sounded politically correct in my mind then I can say it out loud.

"Whatever floats your boat Malik. I'm not one of them low down brothers. Those were just dreams aight."

"I hope this won't affect our friendship El, I thought you knew the whole time."

"Andrea knows? Does my wife know?"

If Andrea knew, I was gonna kick her ass, she could have slipped that info to me damnit. And if my wife knows, that's a whole other story. She's gonna be wondering what I have been doing being out all night with a gay man.

"Andrea knows, but I don't think your wife does. It's not something I announce, especially if I'm gonna be working with them."

He was too calm about this whole thing, and he hadn't said anything about my dreams.

"Did you see that shit! What did I tell you? I knew they would get a touchdown within five minutes of the game! Give me my dough fool!" Malik yelled about the game. I had forgot the game was on.

"Damn. Hold up double or nothing. I bet these fools win by at least twenty." If he wanted to talk about something else that was fine with me.

"You sure? That is easy money right there. It's a

bet."

He said as he shook my hand with a hand shake that lasted a little too long and turned into a mini hand hold. Was he doing what I dreamed of? Not like dreamed of because I wanted it to happen, but dreamed of as in, in my nightmares. You know what they say about the curious cat, unfortunately I had a feeling I was about to be a guest at that cats funeral. For the rest of the night we watched the game, and I lost my money. Damn Vikings. We talked about everything except what we both really wanted to talk about.

"You sure you can drive El?" Malik asked when he saw me stumble out of the sports bar.

"I'll ride. You drive." I said with a slight slur in my words.

We always took one car to the sports bar. He would park his car at my house, then we would leave in my car from there. Gas was way too high and it made more sense that way. Most of the way home it was quite. Besides Young Gunz banging in the speakers, it was silent. Usually when me and Malik ride back from watching the game, we end up arguing about what play we thought was the best, or who we thought was the worst player that night. But not tonight.

"Have you ever even been with a woman? I

mean after your Middle School days, like with a real woman." I asked Malik as we pulled onto 94 West.

"Why you think I'm missing something?" He asked as he turned the music down.

"I'll take that as a no."

"Your wrong, I have. It's just not my thing, you know what I'm saying?"

"I guess. I never really understood why men were like that. No disrespect, but it just doesn't seem right."

"None taken. So when are you coming out the closet?" Malik said.

"Nigga, I ain't R. Kelly! Do I look like I'm trapped in the damn closet? Those were just dreams, as a matter of fact, they were nightmares." I yelled.

"What would you do if I kissed you right now?" Malik said as he pulled the car over. Like he was testing me.

"I would knock you the fuck out. Don't play with me Malik. If you like it that way, then do you. But don't try to get me to come down that path with you. Now come on take me to my damn house."

"I bet you wouldn't hit me El."

"Look, just because you won the first bet, don't

think your luck is gonna follow you on this one. Stop playing Malik, for real, I don't play that gay shit. I only told you about those dreams because number one I thought we were cool like that, and number two I didn't think you were like that. Got me in this damn car like you bought to rape me or some shit! Quit asking me these damn questions, and lets go!"

I was mad now, ready to beat his ass. Don't no man try to test my manhood. Fuck that, I am a man, and I love women. I love my wife. Period. I probably looked like a toddler pouting in my seat, but I didn't care, I was ready to get the hell home. I could see Malik looking at me but I refused to look his way. Then he took my chin into his hands, and forced me to look at him, and just like in those dreams, I couldn't move. He moved in close to my face, so close, I could smell his aftershave. The closer he got, the tighter I balled up my fist, it was the only one of my body parts that wasn't immobilized. He took his tongue and outlined my lips.

I couldn't move anything but my fist. It got tighter with each one of his moves. The closer he got the tighter my fist became. Then he put his lips on mine and kissed me. My fist loosened up and my hand opened up and held the back of his head. This didn't seem right, but it felt right. What was happening to me? Was I drunk? Not that drunk. Was I gay? Hell no. I moved my hand from his head, and returned it to the fist it should have stayed as, and then I knocked his ass out.

"You liked it huh?" Malik said as he wiped the blood from his lips. The lips that were just on mine.

"I told you what would happen Malik. I didn't want to hit you, but you left me with no choice, I told you I wasn't low down."

It has been a long time since I had to punch someone, and my fist was throbbing.

"It's down low fool!" Malik said laughing. How could he be laughing after I just socked his ass?

"Whatever it is, you know what I mean. Don't try no shit like that again Malik."

"El shut the fuck up. You sat there and let me lick and kiss you for more than a minute, and then when your conscious got to you, you hit me. Please, you can fool your friends, and even your wife, but you can't fool me El. Remember I'm your friend. I know you. "

"If you say one word to anyone, I swear I will murder you."

"It's not that serious, what would I get from telling anyone. This can be our little secret El. I'm good at keeping things to myself." Malik said as he sucked the blood from his busted lip.

Not only was I somewhat cheating on my wife, but was I gay? I don't believe it. I wish this was another nightmare. I wish I never opened my mouth about the dreams in the first place. What scares me most, is that Malik was right, I did like it.

Andrea

"You're my angel! Oh Angel." I sang to myself on my way back to my apartment. I loved Anita Baker, especially when she was singing about something I could relate to. I would have never dreamed that I would find love again after Raheem, but I am so happy to say that I did. I am so in love with Javonte that it scares me. He is my best friend. I can talk to him about anything and everything. Being with Raheem for so long, I thought that all relationships were supposed to be the way ours was. I thought I always had to take control, and turn someone into who I wanted them to be. But not with Javonte, he is exactly what I want, and more. When he first told me he loved me, I didn't take it seriously at all, and he could tell. We had only been together for a couple of months and I just always thought that love takes more time then that. But the more time we spent together and the more we talked about our future and feelings toward each other, I realized you can't put a time limit on you feelings. I always thought that Raheem was going to be my first, but I guess I was wrong. I was over due for some loving, and once I found love in Javonte, I knew it was time. I understand that Javonte being my first maybe one of the reasons for my emotional overflow for him, but with the way I feel right now, it doesn't matter to me. Like Lauryn Hill and D'Angelo said, Nothing even matters, and now I finally understand what that means.

"Jay I'm back." I said as I entered my apartment. Jay didn't live with me and Trina, but he was always here. Thankfully Trina didn't mind.

"Come show me the pictures." Javonte said.

He was in the living room playing that damn PS2. We had taken a road trip to Chicago last month, and we finally got around to getting the pictures developed. It was on that trip when I began to open up to Jay. One night he asked me what I wanted in a man, what I wanted from him. I had never really thought someone would ask me that. I had a mental list of all the things I ever wanted from a man. I told him what was number one on my list. I told him that I wanted to be taken care of. Period point blank. All I have ever wanted was to be taken care of. Looking back on our conversation, I think maybe I should have said something a little more insightful, but I didn't feel the need to. He was everything that I wanted, he is everything I need.

At that time he was giving me everything I needed, so when he asked me what I wanted from him, I just thought about what he wasn't giving. Don't get me wrong, he pays for our dates and shit like that. But I was talking in terms of the long run. And in the long run, I want to be taken care of by him. I understand that right now he isn't in the position to take care of me, but in the future he will be. I was just trying to plant a seed, that's all.

"All these, I thought we only had two cameras?" Jay asked.

"These are Trina's. I had remembered seeing some cameras in her room, so when I knew I was going to get our film developed I took hers too. Is she home yet?" I asked.

My sister and I have gotten so close these past months. We're more than family now, we're friends.

"Yeah she's in her room."

"Trina come see the pictures!" I yelled toward her door.

"What pictures?" She asked as she walked into the living room.

"The ones me and Jay took when we were in Chicago. Oh and I got your cameras developed for you too." I said

"Where are they Andrea?" Trina asked sounding a little too frantic about some vacation pictures.

"Right here Trina damn, you'll get your turn." I said jokingly.

"No Andrea, my pictures, from my cameras?

Why did you go through my things anyways?"

"First of all, I was just being thoughtful, second of all what's the big damn deal? You sound like you got something to hide?" I picked up her pictures and ran across the room.

"Come on Andrea, quit playing! Give me my pictures!" Trina yelled as she chased me around the apartment.

"You want them so bad? Come and get them fool!"

I saw she was serious, but that was the best time to mess with her. Seeing her mad cracked me up, especially over some pictures. She could be so dramatic at times.

"Drea you play too much, please give them to me."

She pleaded with me as I ran into the kitchen. Then I slipped on a dish towel and the pictures flew out of my hands, and onto the floor.

"What were you so pressed about Trina? You didn't want me to see pictures of you with Mom?" I said as I held up some of the fallen pictures. Why was she tripping, these pictures were a lot more innocent than the ones Jay and I took?

"Just give me the pictures Andrea." Trina said

while picking up the negatives off the kitchen floor.

"What the fuck is this Trina!" I screamed at her. I couldn't believe what I was seeing. Now it was all making sense. I didn't know what to think as I looked through the pictures of Trina with Nicki. They looked like hoes, dressed up in lingerie and posing like they were lovers.

"Andrea I was gonna tell you. I just didn't know how." Tears were falling from her eyes. She looked as sad as the day I took her in.

"Tell me what Trina? Tell me that you and Raheems girlfriend used to date? Or whatever the fuck yall were doing. Look at you Trina. You look like a damn hoe!"

"Calm down baby. Now what's going on?" Jay asked. He knew I was mad, and needed to chill before I said or did something I'd regret.

"I was gonna tell you once I found out Raheem knew her too, but I just didn't know how to say it, or where to start." Trina said through tears and loud crying.

"Stop crying and tell me what the hell is going on Trina." I wasn't in the mood for no damn sob story, I just wanted to details and I wanted them right now. Straight up with no chaser.

"When I first left home, I was doing real good.

Remember Andrea? I had a car, a place to live and I was going to Community College, everything was going good. Then I met Nicki when I was working at the bookstore at school. She was real nice at first, and we became friends. Then she started telling me about how I could make some real good money, fast money. At first it sounded real good and the money was coming in left and right."

"What were you doing Trina?" I asked scared of the answer she might give me.

"We were escorts."

"You mean a hoe." I said with disgust in my voice.

"No, Andrea I wasn't having sex I swear. We would just go out with these rich men, and they would pay us. We would go to parties and out of town with them, they just wanted some female company."

"That's not that bad baby." Jay said trying to minimize Trina's escorting.

"Shut up Javonte." I snapped "Finish Trina, I know there has to be more to this story."

"After about a year of escorting, Nicki said we would make a lot more money if we started sleeping with these men too. The first time I did it, I couldn't stop crying. Nicki was fine with it though."

"I bet that slut was. Why the fuck would you even consider sleeping with those men? What's wrong with you?"

"I was young Andrea. Anyways, I found that the only way to could handle having sex with those men, was if I was drunk. After a while I got sick of being drunk all the time and Nicki could see that. I was tired of that life and I was about to quit and go back to school. When I told Nicki I was ready to quit she wasn't as mad as I thought she would be, she said it was my choice. At that time I was smoking weed every once in a while, and we decided to smoke to celebrate the fact that I was going back to school. It was Nicki's idea and she was my friend so I didn't think anything of it. Once we started smoking, I started to feel real different, I knew this wasn't the same high I was used to. I asked Nicki what I was smoking and she said it was dirty, and started to laugh."

"Dirty? She laced your shit with that devil Trina? She got you hooked on coke?"

"I didn't think I was gonna be hooked on it, but the next morning when I woke up I was yearning for it and Nicki was right there with the supply. From that day on I was hooked and I did any and everything I had to just to chase my high. Nicki had me sleeping with all types of people, from the riches man to the grimiest nigga off the block. And at that time I didn't care. Nicki found a new hustle in stripping and got me to dance at the club with her. About after a month or so of stripping I told Nicki that I didn't want to do it anymore, and I told her I was going home and getting help. The night that was supposed to be my last night at the club I didn't dance because I was too busy being beat and tortured by Nicki.

She handcuffed me in her apartment and beat my ass everyday and night for days. I was raped by every Tom, Dick and Hakeem, but I was so doped up I didn't feel anything. Once Nicki let me go, she told me that if I ever thought about leaving her, she would find me and make my life a living hell. She said she would make it so bad that I would have no choice but to come back to her. Then she disappeared out of my life. She probably got another young girl working for her now. But once I saw her with Raheem, I knew that something was up, and I just didn't know how to tell you. I was ashamed of what I had allowed myself to get involved in."

I didn't know what to say. I seen my sister in tears and hurting, but I didn't know what to say. All I knew about my sister was that she was hooked on drugs. I never knew the whole story on why it happened. And to find out how and why, that hurts my heart.

"We gotta tell Raheem." I said.

"Why you worried about his ass? If he wants to be with that hoe, then that's on him, that ain't got shit to do with you Drea." Jay said.

"You don't understand Javonte. Nicki is crazy. You don't know what she is capable of." Trina said as she wiped the tears from her eyes.

"Well if you two want to go over there and be all up in that mans business, then I guess I should come to make sure he stays in pocket." Jay said.

"Whatever lets just go." I said.

Trina had said so much, so quick, it hasn't even all sunk in yet. All I know is that Raheem's hoe got my sister hooked on that shit and could have killed her. For all these years, I looked down on Trina, and thought so little of her. I never knew the whole story. I never really wanted to, I thought I knew all I needed to know. I didn't know what I was gonna say to Raheem or what I was gonna do if that bitch was there. All I knew was somebody was gonna get hurt, and it wasn't going to be me.

Raheem

Thank God this is Nicki's last week dancing, I was getting real sick and tired of the stares we would get when we were out together. It's like the whole Twin Cities knew that Nicki danced. And when we would ride past 26th, it's like she had a little fan club. I didn't know what that was about, but when I asked her how she knew all those grimey cats, she said she grew up with them. She hasn't lied to me before, so I doubt she would lie about something like that. Nicki and I have been together for more then eight months and I decided our relationship couldn't go on any further if she was going to continue dancing. She told me that the only reason she was dancing was because of all the bills she had, along with her tuition. She starting crying hysterically and said she hated to dance, but she didn't know what else to do. That was when I decided I had to be a man, and take care of my woman. I made a deal with Nicki that I would pay off all her debts, pay her rent until her lease was up, and after that she could move in with me. I loved Nicki, and I could see the hurt in her eyes when she talked about dancing. She didn't like that life, and I could tell. Little by little Nicki began moving her stuff into my house. I loved my own space, and I loved living alone. I didn't have to worry about anything or anyone but myself, but that is all about to change.

After Nicki told me that she had decided to take

me up on my offer, I did some thinking, and deep soul searching. Nicki is the love of my life, she may act like a mental patient sometimes, and curses like a sailor, but I love her. She takes care of me in ways I never knew I needed to be taken care of. I try not to compare her to Andrea, but that's hard to do. Andrea was my world for most of my life, and besides the games she played, she was perfect. Every once in a while, when Nicki and I aren't quite seeing eye to eye, I long for Andrea. Our relationship was like breathing to me, it kept me going. Even though my breaths aren't as smooth with Nicki, I make sure I carry around a mental inhaler for those times when it's hard to breathe. For the times I mentally back track to Andrea, I just remind my self of the way she left me when I was down, I remind my self of all the mind games. I remind myself that she has moved on.

"Where have you been hiding man?" I asked El. It felt like I hadn't talked to El in months.

"I've been around, just working hard that's all. How's life?" El asked. He was so vague about his hiatus I didn't know what to think. I filled him in on what was going on with me. I told him about Nicki and my plans to move her in with me.

"What the hell is wrong with you? She is a grown ass woman Raheem. You are not her father, you are her man. Support her and take care of her emotionally. Don't go paying that girls debts off. You act like she's your wife, she is your girlfriend, that is all. Nothing more, nothing less. " El said.

This was the first time I had told anyone my plans with Nicki, so I expected that reaction.

"Well that is what I wanted to talk to you about. I was thinking about proposing to her."

"So what? You get a little ass, and now you want to marry this girl? What has gotten into you Raheem? You sound like a damn fool."

"A fool? Just because I love someone, and I want to take it to the next level? That makes me a fool?" I said. I thought I could at least get some kind of support from my boy. I guess I was wrong.

"No, that doesn't make you a fool Raheem. But what does is you falling in love with a damn stripper, then paying off that hoes bills, and moving her in with you. That make you a damn fool. That girl has been stripping for years, if she wanted to get out of it, she could have done it on her own. Now here you come, Captain Save-A-Hoe, talking about paying her bills, and moving her in with you. She was just waiting for the dumbest nigga to make life easier for her, and she got exactly what she wanted. She is playing you man, why can't you see that?"

"First of all, Nicki isn't a hoe. Just because she dances doesn't make her a hoe. And she is not playing me, I brought it up to her. She didn't bring it up. You know what, I thought I could at least get a congratulations from one of my best friends, but I guess I was wrong."

"If it was anyone besides her, then of course I would congratulate you, but it's not, it's her."

"Maybe your right, maybe she is playing me, but I don't see it."

"Just take your time with this girl and keep your money to yourself, and if you can't do that then loan it to her. Write out a promissary note, and tell her you'll help her out until she can find a job and then she can pay you back. Tell her she can keep her apartment for now, and see what she says. If she agrees, then maybe I was wrong and she really wants to get out of it. But if she snaps out, then she just wants a free ride."

"You have a point, but it sounds like game playing, and you know how much I hate playing games El."

"The only one playing a game is her. And the only way to find out if she is that deal, is to tell her about the loan, and not moving her in. I guarantee her true character is bound to show."

"Since when did you become an expert on relationships?"

"Let's just say, I know that love can make you

blind to the truth at times. Love can make a fool out of the best of us." El said.

I never heard him talk like this. Not about love. I was always the one dealing with emotions. He always dealt with the facts.

"Is everything alright with you El?" I asked. I could tell by his tone and content of his conversation, something wasn't right with him.

"Actually Raheem I have been needing someone to talk to. I'm having a problem, but.."

"Open up this hot damn door Raheem!" I heard what sounded like Andrea banging at my door.

"El Let me hit you right back, I think Andrea is banging at my door." I said as I hung up the phone.

What the hell did she want, beating on my door like a mad woman. There are no hard feelings between Andrea and me, so I had no idea what the problem was. I guess I was about to find out.

"What's your problem girl?" I yelled at Andrea as I opened the door to let her and unknowingly, Trina and Javonte in my home.

"Where is that bitch?" Andrea screamed. I had never seen her this upset, and I couldn't dream of what had gotten her to that level.

"Who Andrea? What's wrong with her yall?" I

asked Trina and Javonte, who were just standing at the door way in silence.

"Your bitch Raheem. Nicki, where is she I know she's here!" Andrea said as she ran through my house.

"Will somebody please tell me what was going on?"

"Raheem you stupid mother fucker Nicki is the one that got Trina hooked on that shit. Your precious bitch got my sister stripping, raped, beat and hooked on those damn drugs."

"Andrea how dare you come in my home disrespecting me and my woman. I don't know what has gotten into you, but I advise you to calm the hell down."

"Is that all you heard Raheem? Did you hear me? Nicki got Trina into that nasty world of hers."

Andrea was screaming so loudly I could barely make out what she was saying. After Javonte and Trina got her to calm down, they finally told me the story.

"I don't believe you Andrea." I said. There was no way that was true. I know Nicki. She hated dancing, she told me so herself. Almost every night after work, she would come to me crying about how much she hated it. Not in any way, shape or form could this be true.

"What? You don't believe me? Why would I lie Raheem? What would I gain?" Andrea said with tears in her eyes. I had never seen her cry a day in my life, but not even her tears could convince me that she was telling the truth.

"Andrea, from the first day you met Nicki, you hated her. You hated seeing me happy and with someone other than you. You're jealous, and evil. I know how you are, and how you manipulate people."

"Nigga, she can give a fuck about you and your little relationship with that hoe, she was just trying to look out for our dumb ass. You have known Trina for years, and she thought that you would care enough to listen. But if you don't care, then Andrea you shouldn't care." Javonte said.

"Look boy, this ain't got a damn thing to do with you. You don't know me, or my girl. So I would suggest you getting the hell out my face and my house." I snapped at Javonte.

He had no right to try to tell me about what was going on. It didn't involve him at all. They all had a lot of nerve busting into my house like this.

"Boy!" Javonte yelled.

"Look yall, if he doesn't want to listen then that's on him. Lets just go." Trina said looking at me in disgust. Just as they went for the door, Andrea pulled something out of her pocket and threw it in my face.

"Look at those and then tell me how much of a jealous liar I am."

Andrea said while standing in the doorway. All three of them just stood there, waiting for me to open the envelope. When I opened it, I saw Andrea and Javonte standing in front of Harpo Studios in Chicago.

"What is this? You and your man on vacation Andrea? Why would I want to see this? What does this have to do with anything? See, all you want to do is try to make me jealous of the two of you, and this was what you came up with? I thought that maybe time would change you, I thought that maybe you would grow up a little bit, but I guess I was wrong. Get out of my home now!" I couldn't believe Andrea.

"What do you mean? Give me those pictures." Andrea said as she snatched them from my hands.

"No, these are the wrong ones Raheem. There in the car, I swear just wait until you see what I want you to see, then we will leave, but not until I show you." Andrea said as she ran out to the car.

I don't know what they wanted me to see, or what they could even show me to prove their case. I know how Andrea can get when she wants something. It doesn't matter who she hurts, or who she crosses as long as she gets her way. I remember how she was acting at the barbeque when she first saw me with Nicki. She was acting, just like she would in High School, like a spoiled brat. I heard her tell Javonte someone close to me wasn't going to be around much longer. She said it loud enough for me to hear. I knew what she meant. She was going to do what she had to do in order to get Nicki out of my life. Even though a part of me wanted to see what she had against Nicki, the other part knew that this was just her first attempt to try to break us up.

"Now look." Andrea said as she gave me another envelope of pictures.

"Baby, who's car is that in the driveway? I had to park in the back, and you now how much I hate parking in the back." I heard Nicki say as she came in the back door.

My heart dropped when I heard her voice, not only because I was afraid of what Andrea was going to do to her, but because I had seen the pictures and I couldn't believe what I saw.

El

Damnit! Every time I'm about to come clean about something, I get interrupted. It must be a sign, or maybe it's just not the right time. Maybe I have to get my thoughts together before I try to share them with someone else.

"Was that Raheem?" Mia asked me.

"Yeah and baby you would not believe what he is thinking about doing." I said to my wife.

"I heard you all the way upstairs. Raheem has been tripping lately. Come up stairs I got a surprise for you."

She has been trying so hard for these past couple months to make me happy. She works extra hard at the office to help me so I'm not so stressed, and she works twice as hard at home to make sure I'm happy. Mia has been talking about having a second baby once Laurence turns two, and to tell the truth, I'm not ready for another child. Not right now.

"Wow Mia. You look good."

She did look good. She had finally lost all her baby weight, and she couldn't wait to show it off. She had on a black and pink tight see through lace dress. With black and pink matching stilettos. I must admit my wife was sexy as hell.

"Good enough to eat?" She playfully asked.

"Baby you know how I feel about making love in the middle of the day. I'm tired and I just want to relax right now, can't this wait until tonight. I mean I don't want to disappoint you."

"Since when El? Since a couple of months ago? Back in the day you didn't care what time of day it was, or how tired you were, or how tired I was for that matter. Now all of a sudden you have limitations on when I can make love to my husband? This is bullshit El. All I have done lately was make sure you were happy, and this is the thanks I get?" Mia yelled.

I had never heard her talk like this, I knew this was how she felt, but she would never verbalize it to me. She had become weak over the past couple of years, but now it seems she has her backbone back, and I wasn't prepared.

"Look the truth is I had an appointment to pick you up something special, to show my appreciation for all that you have been doing for me lately, and I wanted to make it there before the shop closed. I have been planning this for months."

I lied. I did have an appointment, but it had nothing to do with Mia. I was going to meet up with Malik. We had been seeing each other for the past couple of months, and he was the reason I didn't like to be with my wife in the daylight. I had passion marks on me in places that my wife was sure to notice. I was living a double life, and I didn't know how to stop, or which side to choose.

"You better not be lying to me El, I swear. I will be able to tell if you were telling the truth, trust me." She said sounding less like a fact and more like a threat.

"I'm not lying baby, you'll see. I'll be back soon." I said as I left my wife standing there in the bedroom doorway. A part of me felt bad, the other part was eager to see Malik.

Those dreams I had been having awoke some feelings and thoughts I never knew existed within me. That night when Malik kissed me, it all made sense. I wasn't gay, just in need of a different kind of love, a love that my wife was unable to give. The love I have for my wife hasn't changed at all, not one bit, but it's like I have two sides to my being. My wife takes care of one, and Malik takes care of the other side. It's hard to explain, mostly because I don't know what's going on myself. Malik and I have an agreement. We won't tell anyone about what is going on between us. If we have to meet up, it has to be at a hotel, not his home and defiantly not my home. He has promised me that he wouldn't say a word to Andrea, ever. Even if we stop communicating, he cannot say one word about our affair.

"What took you so long?" Malik asked. He was sitting at the bar that we decided to meet up at.

"Mia, that's what. She has gotten real mouthy lately Malik. I don't know what her problem is." I said as I took a sip of the beer Malik had ordered for me.

"You know she knows right?" Malik said.

"No, she doesn't. There is no way she even suspects it. Unless you've been running your mouth." I said with a mouth full of complementary peanuts.

"You know I haven't said a word. It's just that from what you have told me about how she has been acting, I can tell she knows something is going on. And I don't mean she knows your gay, but.."

I cut him off.

"Malik I'm not gay, for the fifteenth time, I told you about that shit. Do I look gay?"

"Shit, do I?" Malik snapped back. "Whatever you want to call it El, all I'm saying is that she can tell your seeing someone else."

"You got to talk to her for me Malik. I can't have my wife suspecting anything. Otherwise, she might start following me and shit, and I can't have her find out about us, not like that."

"What you mean I have to talk to her? What do you want me to say, 'Don't worry Mia I know for a fact it's not another woman because it's me, Im sleeping with your husband, oh and by the way can I have a raise?' Be serious."

"Don't play Malik, I am serious, just talk to her and see how she feels about us, I mean our marriage. For real Malik, I don't think I can do this anymore if there is a chance we could get caught." I whispered.

"Whatever El. So what does that mean, we can't sleep together until you know how our wife feels?"

"That's exactly what I mean. Now come help me pick her out something special. I told her I was on my way to go get her a gift, to show my appreciation for her." I said as I got up from the bar

"Can we make a quick stop first?" Malik asked.

I knew where he wanted to go. He wanted to stop at the Hilton Downtown. Even though I told him we couldn't mess around until I knew for sure how Mia felt, I just couldn't resist Malik. Before we went to pick up something for Mia, we made our much needed stop. I made sure to tell Malik to watch where he puts his lips, because of those passion marks he likes to leave. He was a little upset, but those are the breaks when your dealing with someone with a wife. Dealing with Malik was like being with your best friend. He wasn't too girly with me. He was actually a little thugged out at times. If someone saw us walking down the street, they would think we were just close friends, if not brothers, they would never in a million years think that we are lovers. And in some ways I think I did love Malik, not the same way I love my wife, it's a different kind of love.

Andrea

"What are all these people doing in my home?" Nicki said.

"Tell her Raheem. Tell her you what you know." I said staring that bitch in her eyes. I was just waiting for her to look at me the wrong way, to breathe a little but too deep. Just like a lion I kept my eye on my prey.

"Let me handle this Andrea. Nicki, baby can you explain these pictures?" Raheem asked her too calmly. He had evolved into a punk, plain and simple. I couldn't believe my ears.

"They're pictures of me and a dancer at the club baby. What's the big deal?" She nonchalantly said as she looked up at Raheem.

"They told me you were the one that got Trina hooked on drugs Nicki, that you had her raped and beaten? Is this true?" Raheem asked her. He had to be the dumbest person I know, all he had to do was look at the pictures, they told a story of their own.

"What? Who is Trina?" Nicki asked looking at me with a little smile on her face.

"Bitch you think this is a joke? You trying to be funny? You know who Trina is, she's in those pictures with your nasty ass." It took every bone in my body not to jump up and knock that trick out, it took every bone and the fact that Javonte was holding me back.

"Trina? No the girl in this pictures name is T.O., you know like the receiver who is always open."

"What!" I yelled. I tried my hardest to get out of Javonte's grip, but he had too much of a hold on me.

"Nicki, this is Trina in those pictures with you, Andrea's sister. I thought you said you never seen her before, you said you didn't know her, but here you are in pictures with her, kissing on her. Explain that to me."

"I didn't recognize her baby. Look at her compared to her in these pictures. She looks like two different people. It's an honest mistake."

"What about the drugs Nicki, what about the rapes and the beatings?" Raheem asked. What did he think, that she was going to tell the truth? This bitch was trifling.

"I never did anything to hurt T.O. Maybe it was one of the many men she was with. Those men were into some heavy drugs."

"She's lying Raheem!" Trina yelled.

"I don't know what to believe. I can see how she couldn't recognize Trina, I mean she did look a lot different, I don't know what to think." Raheem said looking as sorry as he is was.

"What is wrong with you Raheem? Have you lost your mind, what do you mean you don't know what to believe? Trina is like a sister to you, and you know about the hurt my family has been through because of her drug use. Now we know the reason, your bitch is the reason, and you don't know what to believe?" I couldn't believe what I was hearing.

"Andrea, just go. You have disrespected me for the last time. Get out of my home, I need to think some things out and I don' t have time for your immature comments." Raheem said as he opened the door to kick us out of his home.

He was kicking us out, and letting that trick stay. I always knew that no matter if Raheem and I were together or not, I always knew he would be there. But when I heard his door slam behind us I knew that he wasn't the same Raheem I had grew up with.

The whole way back to my apartment, all I could do was cry. Not just because of the way Raheem treated us, but because I began to realize what my sister had gone through and it hurt me deep in my heart. Just to know that Raheem was laid up with that trick made me sick to my stomach. Whatever attraction I had left for Raheem was all gone, he had become more of a dumb ass then he was before.

"I should have knocked that cat out! I can't

believe you used to be with him. He's a trick for real. I should have knocked his ass out." Javonte went on and on, about what he should have done, or should have said, and I was sick of hearing it.

"Shoulda, coulda, woulda Jay. It's over, plus you don't want any trouble right now. He is gonna get what is coming to him, and it's not up to us anymore to try to save him from that fate." I said to calm Jay down.

I was glad he didn't throw any punches at Raheem. He was about to go into the draft and he didn't need anything coming in between him and getting into the NFL.

"Trina you alright?" I asked my sister. She was so quiet I had forgotten she was in the car. I had no idea what she was going through, but I could see she was hurt.

"I'm fine, seeing Nicki just brought up a whole lot of feelings that I had locked away deep inside. Andrea I'm telling you, without my faith I don't think I would still be here, she really messed me up sis." Trina said trying to hold back tears.

I wanted to make it all better, I wanted to just erase her past for her so she didn't have to hurt anymore. She had gone through so much pain in the past. And to know that I wasn't there for her made me feel lower than low. I was supposed to be her family, I was supposed to be the one that was there when no one else was around, but instead she turned to Nicki.

I can remember one night my sister had called me and said she needed to talk to me, but I was so busy dealing with my friends issues I put her on the back burner. I didn't even care that she said it was important, I didn't care that she said she needed my help, all I cared about was my friends mini drama's and helping them out. After that phone call she called Nicki, and found sisterhood in her. Even though Trina's situation wasn't about me, I felt somewhat responsible. I should have been there for my sister back then and I'll be damned if I make that same mistake twice.

Mia

Does he think I'm stupid? In the past I might have been a little naive, but when you have been left alone, with no ones thoughts but your own, you start to really think about things. Andrea is so wrapped up in Javonte, she hasn't made anytime for me, and when I do finally get to talk to her, all she does is talk about him. Never once does she ask me how I'm doing. I guess she just assumes everything is just peachy.

After too much unwanted alone time, I began to think a whole lot. When I first met El, I was a strong willed young woman, and nobody could tell me anything. But since I put that ring on my finger I have began to lose myself in him. Month by month and year by year, everything I began to do wasn't for me anymore, it was for El. I married El when I was young, so I never really got a chance to hit the clubs, or anything like that. I didn't care though, because I was in love. I am in love and love being El's wife, but there is more to me than just that. I had lost my voice with El. I don't have a say in anything anymore.

From the color of my home, to the layout of my furniture, it was all his idea, with no input from me. I don't like orange walls in the living room. He does. I think it looks like a rotten pumpkin spread onto the walls, but I wouldn't tell him that. And this damn leather furniture, I hate leather furniture. I stick to it in the summer time, or if I'm sitting there for too long, and sometimes it hurts when I get up off of it! But does he care? No, he could careless. But things are about to change. I'm sick of being Mrs. Nice Tamia. I'm sick of working and coming home and working some more, just to have him leave me and the baby almost every night. And when he is here physically, he sure ain't here mentally. He's just like my Father. I really do believe he thinks I'm stupid. He thinks I don't see those marks on his body, in places I haven't been in a while. The nerve of El to go and get a chick on the side, like I'm not all he needs. I don't know how I'm gonna prove it. I should just ask someone who knows him well enough, to know if he is cheating. But first I'm ordering some new furniture and getting these walls painted over. I was thinking a light pink. I know El would hate that, but I love it, and right now that's all that matters.

Raheem

"So why didn't you tell me you knew Trina?" I asked Nicki for what seemed like the eighteenth time.

"Raheem why are you tripping? Like I said before, I didn't recognize her."

We had been arguing ever since Andrea and her posse left. No matter how many times we talk about, it still doesn't make any since to me.

"Why are you lying Nicki?" I said. After hours of talking about it, I began to think back to our first date, when Trina seen me with Nicki. The way they were both acting seemed suspect.

"What do you mean baby? I'm telling you the truth."

"No you're not, I remember when we were at lunch, I remember the way you looked at Trina when you saw her, and I remember how you acted once you found out I knew her. It all makes sense now Nicki." I said a little too late. Andrea and Trina must hate me right about now, but I really didn't know what to think at the time.

"So what if I knew her. It doesn't.."

"Did you have Trina raped and beaten Nicki, did you get her hooked on that shit?" I asked with anger in my voice. Trina was like a sister to me, and I loved her that way. Just to know that the woman I love had something to do with her downfall, made me sick.

"She belonged to me Raheem. You don't understand how it works on the streets. Trina made the choice to be with me, and the things that happened to her were apart of that choice." Nicki said with no emotion.

"Your cold Nicki, you know that. You sat there and lied in my face and now all of a sudden you come clean that they were telling the truth? Get the hell out of my house Nicki. I can't be with you."

"You can't be with me? I'll let you be mad for a couple of days, hell maybe even a couple of weeks, but you are not going anywhere."

"What? Am I supposed to be scared? Well I'm not. Nicki I don't want anything to do with your lying ass. You're dirty and I don't want you anymore."

"Dirty? Fuck you Raheem you dumb ass trick, that's what you are you know that right. I gave you my good head for free, nigga you owe me a couple G's for all those freebies I gave you. You right, I am a hoe, I'm a well paid hoe, and proud of it. Did you really think I made all that money just from dancing? But one thing was true, I was gonna stop. Only because your dumb ass was gonna take care of me!" Nicki said as she laughed.

"Get out Nicki! Now before I call the police!" I threatened her with the cops because I didn't know what she was going to do.

"Call the police, they pay the best anyways. As a matter of fact I'll do you a favor, I'm gonna leave Raheem, but just know it's not over." Nicki said as she slammed the back door and started laughing like a damn hyena.

That bitch was crazy, I can't believe what just happened. I thought I knew her, I thought I loved her. I do love her, but not that crazy part, I love the part she showed me. I don't know who that woman was that just left, that's not who I fell in love with. Now I got to think of how I'm gonna apologize to Andrea and Trina. I made an ass out of myself by choosing Nicki over their word. If I were them, nothing I could say would lift the hate cloud from my head. I just hope they are in a forgiving mood.

~Sweet Juice, Bitter Aftertaste~

Andrea

"What do you want Raheem?" I asked. I haven't heard from him in over a month since he kicked me out of his house. Now all of a sudden he's calling.

"I know I'm probably the last person you want to hear from right now. I just needed to take sometime and think things through before I tried to apologize about how I acted. I am really sorry about what happened that night Andrea. I guess you could say I was blinded by love."

"What about the love for Trina, not to mention the love for me. I thought that at least we were friends Raheem. Me and Trina were and still are really hurt with the way you treated us. I can't believe you choose that.."

"Look Andrea. I don't want to get into that again. You have every right to be mad at me, I understand. I just wanted to let you know that I was sorry, and I feel really bad about what I did."

I could tell he was sorry. A part of me was glad he waited so long before calling me, because who knows what I would have said to his ass. I know Raheem and I know that when he is in love, he can love a little too hard at times. And all logic is out the window when he gets like that. I should know. I'm trying to work on myself, and one thing I need to work on is holding onto things. I have learned to let go, especially if I have no control over it. So even though I was tight at Raheem for what he did, I forgive him, and hold no hard feelings toward him.

"I accept your apology Raheem."

"That's it?" Raheem asked.

"What do you mean?" I was confused.

"I mean, your not going to cuss me out, and tell me how stupid I am for choosing her over you and Trina?"

"For what? Sounds to me like you already know." I said.

I just didn't have it in me to tell him about his self. He knew he was wrong, and that's all that mattered.

"Raheem we're having a draft party for Javonte next week at Mia and El's house. You're more than welcome to come. Trina will be there just incase you wanted to tell her something." I hinted.

"Yeah, I'll be there. Thanks for the invite Andrea."

"No problem, just make sure if you bring a date, that they have been evaluated by a professional before they step foot in the house."

"You got jokes. I'll see you next week Andrea." Raheem said before he hung up.

"Who was that?" Javonte asked.

"You know who that was, you were in my mouth the whole time I was on the phone." I snapped back. I hated when he asked dumb questions. He knew I was talking to Raheem.

"It's kinda late for that nigga to try to apologize, don't you think?" Jay said. I could tell he wanted to argue, and I just didn't want to go there right now.

"I guess Jay." I said hoping he would leave it alone.

"So why did you invite him to my party Andrea? The party is for friends and family, and he isn't either one."

"Look he was probably going to be there anyway since its gonna be at his boy's house, so its no big deal. I'm not gonna hold on to what happened, I accepted his apology so now we can move on."

"Did you talk to them about the party yet?" Javonte asked.

With the way he changed the subject I could tell he could sense I was not in the mood for a petty argument, and I'm so glad he picked up on it.

"No I'm on my way over there right now to talk

to Mia."

It was kinda funny that we had already invited some people to their house, and I haven't even gotten their permission yet. I doubt its gonna be a problem though, I just hope they don't have anything going on.

"Andrea I really appreciate all the work your putting into this draft party. It really means a lot to me." Javonte said. He was such a sweetheart.

"I just don't want you to worry about anything right now baby. You have your finals to worry about, and plus this draft. I know how stressed you must be, I just wanted to lighten your load a little, that's all."

Even though planning his party had me a little stressed, I was okay with it. I couldn't imagine how he was feeling right now.

"I wanted to talk to you about something before you left." Jay said as he motioned for me to sit next to him on the bed. He was playing that damn PS2 like always, but he at least paused the game to talk to me.

"What's up baby?"

"Now you know I really want to play for Minnesota right?"

"Yeah I know."

"Well, my agent called me the other day and told me that some out of state teams were looking at me too."

"Ok?" I didn't know what he was trying to say.

"And there is a chance that I could get drafted to an out of state team, even though I want to go with the Vikings."

"So what are you trying to say baby?"

"I'm just giving you a heads up, that's all."

A heads up to what? That other teams are looking at you? That you might have to move out of town? That if you do move out of town we can't be together, or that you don't want to be together? I hated to assume things but he was leaving things way too open.

"Are you trying to tell me something, because if you are I wish you would just say it?"

"I know you have your work and everything going on here, and of course your family and friends, but if I have to leave out of state, I mean I don't want you to have to leave everything you know just for me." Jay said stuttering.

"Jay you know I hate it when you do that, what are you trying to say." I snapped at him.

I hated when he rambled on just making statements, not stating any facts. What was I supposed to do with what he was saying?

"Andrea, I shouldn't have brought it up to you yet, because I don't quite know how to word it, just know its not a bad thing. I mean some people might look at it as a bad thing, but it's like a growth thing to me. I guess. I don't know, just go talk to Mia, and we will talk later, once I have my thoughts in order."

"I'll see you later Jay." I said as I left out of the room.

I didn't know how to feel about his rambling on. What was he talking about, and why was it so hard for him to verbalize? My mother told me that I should never mess with a ball player, because once they get a little press, their heads get too big to carry. I bet that is exactly what's going on with him. He's thinking about how big he's gonna get, and will have the opportunity to have any woman he wants. Why just have one, when you can have anyone? I hate when people leave me hanging with my own thoughts, about their thoughts. Then I get all confused and start reacting on my assumptions. I'm just gonna clear my mind, and expect the worst. That way I can't be too upset. Hopefully.

Mia

I can't wait to see Andrea, it seems like forever since we talked. I mean besides idle chit chat at work, we haven't really gotten a chance to really talk. Plus I want to show her the necklace El bought for me from Tiffany's. Well one of the many items he got for me. I was so sure he was lying about having a surprise for me. I almost passed out when he came home with six gift bags from Tiffany's. He said he couldn't decide, so he just bought everything he thought I would like. From rings to necklaces to key chains, if it was at the store, it was in those bags. After being showered with all those gifts, I didn't know what that to think. All that alone time had me thinking things that were probably not even happening.

After I talked to Raheem about my assumptions, I realized I was just tripping. I know El would never even think about stepping outside of our marriage for another female. But one thing I didn't imagine with all that time to myself, was the fact that I had lost parts of myself in this marriage. Without saying a word to El I hired a designer to help me redecorate my home. One weekend while El was on some business trip, I changed every single thing in this house. From that ugly ass paint on the walls, to the place mats on the tables. Everything now had my touch, and I loved it. When I was finished, I felt a part of myself was reborn, and it felt good. El wasn't as mad as I thought he would be. He just told me if I didn't like something I should have let him know. But hey, what's done is done.

"Hey girl I have missed you!" I screamed when I opened the door to see my friend.

"Girl please, you see me almost everyday at work." Andrea said as she plopped down on my new suede couch. I loved it. At least I don't stick to it when it's hot.

"You know what I mean, we haven't really had a chance to talk, I mean really talk. So how's life." I asked.

"Forget about me, what the hell happened to all yall's furniture. It was brand new." Andrea said as she looked around and seen how much everything had changed.

"I just decided it was time for a change that's all."

"So what happened to the old stuff?"

"I had put it in storage, cause like you said it was new. Then El said I should give it to Malik, since he was in need of some new stuff for his place."

"What? You didn't think of me first? Malik don't need shit. He just got all new stuff about a year ago. Why would El volunteer Malik, before me I just don't get it?" Andrea said. I could tell she was mad, but there was nothing I could do about it. From what I knew Malik was in need, and I had no reason to doubt my husband.

"Well there is still some extra stuff in storage, and you are more than welcome to it." I said trying to make it a little better.

"Cool with me." Andrea said smiling.

"So I heard about Raheem's girl, you know he was wrong for the way he treated you two."

"Girl I don't even want to go there. You know he called me today and said he was sorry, and that he was wrong for what he did. I just accepted what he had to say and decided to move on." Andrea said. She had changed so much in this past year. I don't know what or who has gotten into her, but I hope he stays around.

"So how are you and Jay doing?" I asked. I thought they were the cutest couple, so loving.

"That's what I wanted to talk to you about." Andrea said before she asked me if she could have a draft party for him at our house. Of course I didn't mind, she was my girl, and if her man needed some support then I would gladly help out.

"Thank you so much Mia. I hope you don't mind all the press in your house."

"Not at all, I just have to make sure I lose the ten pounds that the camera is gonna add."

"So where is El, I haven't smacked him around in a minute?" Andrea asked.

Her and El were like brother and sister. I was so lucky to have a friend that got along so well with my husband. El hates my model friends. Andrea is the only one he really took the time to get to know.

"He has been hanging with Malik like crazy. Everyday I swear they are out at the bar, or if they aren't out they are here playing cards or watching the game. It's like Raheem Number Two."

"Really?" Andrea asked.

"Yeah, I don't mind though just as long as they stay out the damn strip clubs and night clubs. Other than that I'm fine with them hanging out all the time, it's just sometimes I just wish we had more alone time."

"Have you told El that?"

"No, I haven't, not yet."

"Maybe you should tell him how you feel Mia. You and I both know El ain't no mind reader, and he won't know what's wrong unless you tell him." Andrea said.

"You're right. So have you and Malik been

hanging out any, or has he done you like El has done me?"

"As a matter of fact, I really haven't talked to Malik as much. He says he's busy, but I didn't even know he and El were hanging out like that. So other than him not being around as much, how is everything else going?" Andrea asked.

She was so caring, and always wanted to make sure my marriage was doing okay. When we were younger, she was always the one talking about getting married, being in love and shit like that. It's kinda funny that I was the one married, and she wasn't. I never even thought I would get married, let alone have a son. It's funny how things work out.

"You want to know something funny, I thought El was cheating on me for a while. I'm over it now, but if you asked me a couple of weeks ago, I would tell you for a fact he had someone on the side."

I shouldn't have told her that, and by the look on her face, I wish I hadn't. She just spaced out, and was looking right through me.

"Andrea did you hear me?" I asked. "Andrea!" I said a little louder and snapped my fingers in her face.

"What made you think he had someone on the side?" She asked me, but it didn't feel like she was talking to me. She spoke with a monotone voice, and I could tell something was wrong. If I didn't know any better, I would think that she was sleeping with El.

"I mean I seen passion marks on his body, and he has just been acting really weird. But I think I was just tripping. Girl let me show what he got me from Tiffany's." I said as I ran upstairs to get the bags.

"These are nice, real nice. Mia, has El said anything to you that would make you think he was cheating?" She asked.

I had tried to change the subject, but she still wanted to talk about what I knew. The more we talked about it, and the more questions she asked,the more I began to believe that El was sleeping with someone else. My best friend. I knew she loved us both, but I didn't understand why she was pressing the subject. I had already told her it was probably nothing, but she just kept going. Making me tell her instances over and over again. Like she was trying to see how much I knew. Something just didn't feel right. After she left, I began to back track their relationship, and it was all making sense. Andrea once told me that she had a crush on El back in High School, and El once told me the only person he would even consider having a threesome with would be Andrea. It was in my face the whole time. I was just too dumb to see it.

Raheem

I'm so glad she forgave me. Even though her and Trina forgave my actions, I still felt a little weird about being here. I was invited as a friend, but I didn't feel like much of a friend to either of them. I can see Andrea has matured so much from the way she used to be. I guess Javonte was all she needed to bring that out in her. He brought out something in her I couldn't. Being here at his draft party, makes me feel kinda funny. I'm her ex man, here to support her and her new man. I feel so out of place. Looking at them, so in love with each other, makes me wish I was in his shoes. Just for one minute, that's all I need, just one minute with Andrea. I miss her so much, it hurts, and seeing them together just pushes that knife deeper into my heart. I think that being alone has something to do with it. It's like I have no one to long for, or care for in that way. So that leaves me no choice but to long for what I had in the past. And since I have blocked the memory of Nicki completely out of my mind, Andrea is all I seem to revert back to. Every time I see her, I just want to pull her aside and tell her how I feel, but I can't. I have to respect the fact she is in love right now, even if it's not with me.

"El man what's up?" I said a little too overly excited. I was just so happy to see my boy. I needed something to get my mind off of Andrea.

"Nothing much man, how have you been. I haven't seen you in the office much, you still on vacation?" El asked.

"Yeah, this is my last week. I just needed sometime off. You know what I mean? How have you been? You and the wife aight?" I asked.

"We're fine. Why do you ask?"

"Mia came over to my house the other day, asking me all types of questions about you."

"What types of questions?"

"Is El cheating on me type of questions." I answered.

"What did you say?"

"What should I have said?"

If someone told me my wife was asking my friends if I was cheating on her, "What did you say?" would not be my first response. El had been acting funny lately, but I thought it was just one of his moods, just prolonged.

"No! You should have said hell no!" He snapped.

"Well I did. Even though we haven't talked like we used to, I still told her no."

"What does us talking like we used to have to

do with the question of if I am cheating on my wife?" El asked in a tone I wasn't too familiar with, and with way too much attitude.

"I'm just saying, I don't know what your doing, I just hope you're not doing what she thought you were."

"Well I'm not. Look I'll be right back." El said as he rushed over to the front door and peered out the window like he was waiting on someone.

I don't know what has him so jumpy lately, but he is not the same El I used to know. It's funny when you grow up with someone, you think you know them. I mean how could you miss something when your always around them? But by the way El has been acting, I now know, that no matter how long you might have known someone, you never really know them. Andrea used to say, "People only show you what they want you to see, so don't think you ever really know someone, until you have seen both sides." Now I understand what she meant. All these years El was showing me one side, the side of him he wanted me to see. Now I see his other side showing, and I think I know why he hid it from me in the first place.

El

I thought that expensive ass jewelry would kill her suspicions, but I guess I was wrong. Malik was right, Mia did know something was going on. I just wish she would have talked to Malik instead of Raheem about it. By the way he was acting, I doubt if what he said to her was at all convincing. I wish Malik would hurry up and get here.

"Waiting for someone?" Andrea asked. She had snuck up behind me.

"Yeah, well not really. I'm just waiting on the liquor to get here."

"If you say so." She whispered in my ear. I could feel my wife's eyes staring at me and Andrea. Either I was just paranoid, or my wife knew what was going on, and had sent Andrea over to shake me up.

"What are you talking about Drea?" I asked her.

She was so close to me, I could tell she was trying to intimidate me. Even though I was trying my hardest to keep my cool, her tactics were working. My wife was staring so hard, it felt like she was reading my mind, either that or putting a root on me.

"Nothing, just talking. Make sure you're around when the draft starts. We want to make sure everyone is in there."

She said as she skipped off. Maybe it was just my mind playing tricks on me. When you have a guilty conscious that tends to happen a lot. One thing I didn't imagine was the way my wife was staring at Andrea and me. Something wasn't right. When I looked up, she was gone. My eyes finally tracked her down talking to Raheem. I just hope they weren't talking about me.

"Where have you been?" I said as I ran out to Malik's car.

"What is your problem El? I'm only five minutes late. Did I miss something?"

"Yeah you missed me getting questioned by Andrea, and mean mugged by my wife. Did you tell Andrea anything?" I asked. I trusted Malik, and I just hope he didn't say anything. We had made a promise to each other, and it would break my heart if he broke it.

"Of course I didn't. You just feel bad that's all. Calm down. Don't draw attention to yourself. Even if they do suspect something, you can't give them a reason to keep those suspicions going." Malik said as he put his hand on my shoulder to comfort me. He saw I was a little wound up. He quickly removed his hand, once he realized we were in front of my home which was full of people.

"Here carry this in, so at least they know you

had a reason for running out here like a crazy person. You really need to calm down El, your just drawing attention to yourself."

He was right. It was all in my head, but I still needed to make sure my wife had those thoughts of me cheating out of her head.

"Finally the real drinks are here!" Andrea yelled as we entered the door. Talk about drawing attention.

"Malik, I need you to talk to Mia." I whispered.

"Why El? She is fine, quit making something out of nothing. Plus you already said she talked to Raheem. Just let it go."

"Raheem didn't say what needed to be said. I need you to talk to her. She knows something. Either you talk to her to calm her and my nerves, or we are going to have to cool off for a while"

"My car overheated on the way here, can you come out and check it out with me, don't worry it wont take too long, I just want to make sure its safe enough to drive home." Malik said loud enough so whoever was within three feet of us could hear.

"Yeah make it fast. I don't want to miss the draft." I said as we headed out to his car.

"What's wrong Malik?" I asked. I knew it had to be something.

"I'm sick of this shit El. I'm sick of being the big gay secret!" Malik said with his hands on his hips and his Mothers tone in his voice.

"Malik, what is your problem. Don't act brand new now. You knew that I had a wife, and you knew I would never go public about us, so now what's the problem?"

"The problem is, this is bullshit. I'm better than this. You got me sneaking around with you at work, in hotels, shit even in your car. I deserve better El, I really do. I thought I could just sleep with you and be done with it, but now my feelings are involved and I can't keep living like this. I love you El, and I can't tell a soul about who has me on cloud nine everyday. When someone asked me why I'm so happy, I say no reason. And I'm sick of you not being a reason El. You are real to me, and so are my feelings for you. This may just be about you getting a different kind of nut, but its more than that to me. Its deeper El, and it hurts me that you don't see it that way."

"Malik I feel the same way as you, but what do you want me to do? I'm stuck."

"No, you're not, your gay, and I want you to just get over what everyone is going to think about you and be gay. That's what I want."

"Then what Malik? I leave my wife, leave my son. Get shunned by her family and not to mention my own family. I'll lose my friends and most likely my job. And what am I suppose to do after I leave everything I know, you want me to run away with you to San Francisco?"

"This isn't a joke El."

"I'm not joking, not one bit. This is my life, and no matter how I feel about you I can not and I will not give that up. I'm sorry Malik."

"I'm sorry too, El. Sorry I ever let myself fall in love with someone like you." Malik said as he walked back toward the house.

"So what does this mean?"

"It means your wife has nothing more to worry about. She won't have to guess about what is going on with you anymore." He said as he walked into the house.

I don't know what he meant by that, but what I did know is that I felt terrible. I loved Malik, I really did, but he should have known there was no way we could get too serious. I understand you can't put restrictions on your feeling sometimes, but there is nothing I can do about that.

When I walked into the house, I saw Malik talking to Mia. I don't think he would risk his job or life for that matter and tell Mia about us. And by the looks of things he wasn't. They were laughing and joking so I knew he didn't say anything, but when I saw them go onto the patio my heart sank. Why did they need to be away from everyone? What were they talking about? What was he saying to her?

Andrea

I hope I'm wrong I really do, but it just doesn't seem right to me. When Mia told me about Malik and El hanging out, I really didn't think too much of it. But when she started telling me about the furniture and the fact that she saw some hoe marks on him, that's when it all made sense. I kept telling myself that it couldn't be true. But by the way those two are acting tonight, I don't know. El has always seemed a little metro sexual, but never in a million years would I think he was bi sexual.

He does have his gay moments. Like when his hands stay on his hips for a little too long. Or when his neck sways a little too much. But I always thought that was just El having one of his mood swings. That's another thing, it never seemed strange to me until now, but what kind of man has mood swings? I can't bring it up to Mia until I know for sure. I think El can tell I think something is going on, because when I was talking to him at the door he began to sweat like a pig. Even though pigs don't sweat, you know what I mean. I'm trying not to think too much about their business, not tonight. Tonight is my man's night, and I have to make sure my attention is on him tonight.

"I wish you could have been there." I said to Javonte. He was a little tight because his agent didn't tell him about the tickets to the draft until last week, and by that time it was already too late for him to reschedule his finals.

"I know, but I'm glad I got a chance to be here with my family and friends instead." Jay said.

I didn't know if that was for me or for the cameras. I was so glad we decided on holding the party here at Mia's house, because there was no way all these reporters could have fit in my apartment. And defiantly not in Jay's studio, me and him could barely fit in there. I'm just glad I wore my good hair and did my Crest White strips, cause these cameras are all up in my grill. I could get used to being on his arm like this. Getting all this attention and not doing any of the work. I just had to make sure I didn't get too comfortable on his arm. He hasn't said anything to me about what he was trying to tell me that day. And just by how he has been acting, I don't think its gonna be something I want to hear. He has been so distant this past week. Part of the reason maybe because of what's going on with the draft, but still something doesn't feel right.

"Ok everyone be quiet I think Javonte might be getting picked up next!" His agent announced. Everyone was crowded around the big screen TV in the living room. It was so quite you could hear a mouse poot. First Tampa picked, then Baltimore, then Saint Louis, then about ten more teams. We sat there for about an hour just waiting. I was so nervous, you would have thought I was gonna be drafted. Then finally it was Minnesota's turn. Even though they had about five players to pick, I was waiting and praying they said Jay's name first. But they didn't. We had to wait for what seemed like a lifetime, then finally it was Minnesota's turn again. I had my fingers crossed on both hands, but when I looked over at Jay, he was looking as if he could careless. His mind was somewhere else.

"We the Minnesota Vikings pick, Javonte Chamberlain of the University of Minnesota!" The coach announced.

The whole house burst into a loud cheer, almost simultaneously. We yelled and toasted each other for about a good ten minutes. I was so happy Jay got drafted into the NFL, but I was more thrilled that he was staying here. Jay was doing interview after interview, and I didn't want to interrupt. After all that jumping around I thought it was about time to do a weave check. I went into the dining room and checked myself out. I didn't know it until now, but I had been crying. I don't cry, as a matter of fact I hate to cry, but I was crying. I was so happy for Javonte that it actually brought tears to my eyes. I just hoped my tears of joy wouldn't become tears of pain. I had a gut feeling that he was gonna break up with me now that he was playing in the League. My gut has failed a few times lately, I just hope this was one of them.

"Andrea come out here, he is about to make a statement and he wants everyone to hear it." Javonte's Mom said.

She was one of the sweetest women I had known. I had never really done too well with Mothers, but Jay's Mom was so down to earth it was hard for me not to like her. I made sure I had my video camera, and then went into the living room. When I got in there, his whole family was sitting on one side and he was sitting right next to them. It was so cute. It looked like a little press conference. I saw a chair next to him, but I wasn't family so I didn't want to sit there, plus it looked like it was for his agent cause it was sort of standing out.

"Give me this camera and go up there and sit down." His agent said to me, and before I knew I was sitting up there with the rest of his family. Luckily I did my weave check, cause it seemed like all eyes were on me.

"First of all I just want to thank everyone for coming out and supporting me. It's just good to know that after all my hard work, long nights and determination that it all paid off." Javonte said as he started his speech. My cheeks were hurting so bad. I just couldn't stop smiling. I was so happy for him. He was finally where he dreamed of being. He went on to thank his teammates, and his friends. Then he thanked each family member, one by one and I was the only one left up there who he hadn't addressed yet.

"And last but not least I want to thank my girl Andrea for helping me through my final and hardest year. Without her, I don't think I would have been able to keep my cool through this stressful time. So from the bottom of my heart I thank you." He said. I felt so special. He was sweet. I thought he was done but to my surprise he kept going.

"Andrea, I never knew I could love this way until I met you. Even though we didn't start off in a fairytale type of way, I just want to make sure we continue on that way. You are my best friend and I love you with all my heart. I want nothing but the best for you, and you deserve nothing less. I wanted to do this along time ago, but I wasn't sure I could give you everything you wanted and needed in life. Now that I have a career in the League I know I can take care of you the way a man should. Tonight will be the one of the best nights of my life if you will agree to wear my ring and be my wife." Javonte finished on one knee and looking up at me for an answer. I couldn't believe this was happening.

"Yes!" I yelled as I kissed him and hugged him as tight as I could, but not before I checked that rock out. Damn! A midget with one leg and two teeth could have proposed to me with that ring, and I would have said yes. I said yes before I could even register what was going on. I didn't know what else to say, I mean all eyes were on me. Not that I had a reason to say anything besides yes. When I looked up after all the excitement, the first person I saw was Raheem. He was standing in the corner away from everything. He wasn't looking at me, but he was staring my way. He was just staring into space, he had a look on his face like someone had died. From a distance I could see a tear fall from his face. He wiped it before anyone else noticed, and before I got a chance to go over there, he had left the party. Even though I had it all, it felt like everything my heart desired had just walked out that door.

Mia

I didn't want to believe it, but I saw it with my own eyes. My best friend and my husband, this could not be happening. I decided to keep my eyes on the both of them that night, and like a hawk I watched. I saw them together and away from the rest of the party, like they were hiding something. They were whispering to each other and standing way too close for comfort. Right in my face and in my own home. How could I be so stupid as to trust any female around my husband, even if it was my best friend. She doesn't care about anyone but herself. And I'm starting to see her true colors. It's not enough that she has a football star, but she has to have my husband too? Andrea has always been jealous of me, for as long as I can remember. She never said or even acted envious, but I could see it in her eyes. When Malik came over to talk to me at the party, it was like he could sense something wasn't right. After I let him know how I was feeling, he guaranteed me that nothing was going on between El and Andrea. Then as he walked away I started to think. Malik was probably just covering up for his friends. I can't trust anyone. Andrea probably planned the whole thing out. It's all a big game to her, but as Little Flip would say, Game Over!

Raheem

I had to take another week off from work after that party. When I saw Andrea with Javonte's ring on her finger, it felt like a part of me had died. I knew I still loved her, but I never knew it could hurt so bad. I just feel empty inside. For days after the engagement I cried like a baby. I can't even cry tears anymore, now I just sit there and stare into space. It was like no matter what happened, we would be together. When we would break up, I would consider it just time apart. Even though with this last break we both moved on further than we had in the past, there was still something telling me we would end up together. That voice died once she accepted Jay's proposal. No matter how much it hurts, I'm just happy that she has what she wants. Jay and I haven't talked since that night at my house, so I was surprised when he called me and asked me to meet up with him.

"What's good baller?" I asked as I greeted Jay.

"Chillin man. Thanks for meeting me here Raheem." He said. Javonte had really changed since the last time I seen him. He had on so much shine, I had to shield my eyes. He was defiantly living up to the baller expectations. Physically at least.

"Before you go any further, I just want to apologize for the way I acted that night. I never really got a chance to talk to you after the whole thing went down."

"Water under the bridge. Beside we got more important things to focus on." He said as he took a sip of his Ice Tea.

Just as he was about to finish, I saw someone's refection in the mirror behind him. I wasn't wearing my contacts, so it was hard to see at first. But once I finally got a chance to focus, I swear I saw Nicki walking away. This wasn't the first time I saw her, she was in my dreams every night. That chick was haunting me in my dreams, and now I was starting to see visions of her. I had to snap out of it once I saw Jay starring at me.

"You okay? Did you hear anything that I said?" Jay asked. I had seen him talking, but once my mind drifted off his words were on mute.

"My bad, what were you saying?"

"I was telling you about the party I'm throwing. Its gonna be off the chain. It's a men only after dark party. You know, just to celebrate my draft and my engagement. My boy had booked some dancers from New York, but that fell through. So I was wondering if you had any connects on the stripper scene? Anyone but that crazy bitch you were messing with." Jay finished.

"Honestly I don't have any connections with

any strippers, that's a road I'll never go down again."

"It's all good." Jay said with his mouth full of popcorn.

"So how are you and Drea doing?" I asked.

I don't know why I asked. I didn't want to know how they were doing. Not that I didn't care, its just that it would hurt too much to hear, right now at least.

"We're good, real good." He said. Good short and sweet. Not too much info just the way I needed it.

Jay and I talked and ate lunch together. It was the first time we were together, without having Andrea around. At first it didn't feel right, I mean me getting all buddy buddy with my ex's fiancé. But after I pushed my emotions to the side, I found out that Jay was a pretty good guy. He really seemed to love Andrea, and that put me a little at ease. The last thing I wanted was for her to get hurt, but by the looks of things, Jay wasn't someone who would even consider doing anything to hurt her. Jay was real down to earth, and unlike most athletes, he was very humble.

"Someone just handed me this flier Jay. You think we can book these girls for tonight?" Jay's friend came into the restaurant and handed the flier to Jay.

"We'll give it a try." He said as he finished his lunch.

Even though people pass out fliers like crazy downtown, it all seemed too good to be true. Usually people are advertising some new club night, or trying to sell their homemade CD, but I've never heard of a strip club passing out fliers in the middle of the day. Maybe I was just putting too much thought into this whole thing. Stranger things have happened, I should know.

"I better see you there tonight Raheem. Don't worry about driving. I'll have the stretch hummer pick you up."

"Doing it big huh?"

"It's the only way I do it! Holla." Jay said as he and his boy walked away.

This party seemed like exactly what I needed. I haven't had much time to just chill with the guys, since El has been missing in action. I was looking forward to tonight. Even though Jay seemed like a real cool cat, I was mostly looking forward to keeping an eye on him. Something was telling me, something about him wasn't right. I was hoping it was the emotions talking and not the facts this time.

El

Now it seemed as though the tables have been turned and now Malik is the one avoiding me. He won't take any of my calls and he refuses to meet up with me anymore. I don't know what to do. I tried flowers and candy, but I guess that stuff only works with my wife because Malik wasn't budging. Plus he had talked to my wife for what seemed like forever and I have no clue what he told her. All I knew is since their little talk she had been keeping a close eye on me. If he wanted to play dirty, that was fine with me.

"Malik can I see you in my office please?" I asked.

I said it after a meeting, that way he had no choice but to obey me. He couldn't ignore me in front of co workers. It wouldn't look right.

"What?" Malik said as he closed my office door behind him.

"Sit down." I said.

"El what is it, I have work to do."

"Work that I gave you to do, don't forget you work for me Malik." I said as I lit the tip of my Cuban.

"Are you trying to threaten me El?" Malik asked.

"Just hear me out Malik. I'm sorry about the things I said, and about how I treated you. I was wrong but I just want to make it right. Just give me a chance and I promise I'll.."

"You'll what El? Leave your wife, come out to your friends and family?" He snapped back.

"You know I can't do that.."

He cut me off again.

"Well then we can't do this El."

"Malik I need you in my life right now, just give me time. This whole thing is new to me, maybe once I get used to it then maybe.."

"Maybe what? You'll leave your wife, and come out to your family and friends?" He was repeating himself. I was trying so hard to keep my cool. I wanted this so bad, and I didn't want my temper to ruin it for me.

"Well like I said if you can't do that, then I can't do this." He said as he got up and headed towards to the door.

"How are you liking that raise I gave you? You almost make what I take home, almost six figures. Must feel good huh? Just think, you weren't making a fourth of what you are making now. That corner store wasn't paying you like I pay you, was it? And I doubt without references from a big company like us that you'll even get a modeling gig that doesn't involve underwear under five dollars. How much were you making? Four or five hundred a month!" I didn't want to play dirty but he left me no choice.

"Is that a threat?" He asked as he slowly walked back into my office, and closed the door he was so eager to exit from.

"No, I'm just advising you that if my needs aren't met, then your stomach won't be fed, at least not by me. I hired you, why couldn't I fire you?"

He sat there and looked at me with the most evil look I had ever seen. But his looks didn't affect me, not one bit. We sat there, both staring at each other, for about two minutes without any words being said. Just looks being exchanged, and internal thoughts taking root.

"Okay El, you know I love my money way too much, and I can't have that taken away." He said exactly what I expected him to. I knew his money was too near and dear to him and that he would do whatever he had to do to keep that money coming in.

"Now that sounds like the Malik I know. So where do we celebrate this reunion?" I asked already knowing the answer.

"Where else? The Hilton Downtown."

"I'll have a surprise for you." I told Malik.

"Me too." He answered back as he left my office. I knew what my surprise was for him, but I couldn't imagine what his could be for me.

Andrea

"You sure your gonna be okay in this apartment all alone?" I asked Trina.

"Andrea don't worry about me. I'll be fine. I'm the oldest not you, you seem to forget that from time to time." Trina said as she threw a pillow at my head.

I was packing up my things and getting ready to move in with Javonte. Within three weeks after he got drafted, he got a house. Well not a house, he got a condo. But it's as big as a house. I was getting my grown women on, and loving it. I still couldn't believe I was getting married. We decided to wait at least a year before the actual wedding ceremony. That didn't stop me from planning everything in my head right now. From the colors I wanted, to the bridesmaids dresses. I always thought Mia would be my maid of honor. I was hers. But lately she has been treating me like shit, and I have no idea why. With everything that was going on, I didn't have the time or energy to think about it. Mostly because it made me kind of sad. I didn't know what was going on with her or if it even had anything to do with me. All I knew was that when I got engaged and reached out for my friends hand she pulled away from me. That hurt. Once I get settled, then I'll have a talk with her. But right now I'm just focused on this move.

I am trying to move as much stuff as I can

before Jay's party tonight. He told me this was a men only type of event, and I know what that means. I'm okay with the fact that there will be strippers there. I trust Jay. Plus they will be there for his boys, not him. Even though he has been acting real different since he got drafted. I trust him. He's starting to hang with the other players now, and its starting to get to his head. Like the other day when I asked him where he was going. Instead of telling me like he usually does, he through a credit card at me and told me to go shopping. Granted I took it and did what he asked of me, but that's not the point. He doesn't think he has to tell me his whereabouts anymore. But besides little things like that, everything is perfect. When I do get a chance to spend time with Jay, I can tell he still loves me the same. I think maybe the stress of having to live up to the ball player's image is starting to get to him. I just wish he would see I'm not looking for him to be anything other than himself.

"Hey Leak. What's up?" I said to Malik. I was so glad he called. I had told him earlier at work I needed him to help me bring some things over to the new house.

"I'm around the corner, come down stairs." He said. I had most of the stuff waiting outside. I hated the whole moving process and I couldn't wait to get this over with.

"Thanks for helping me Malik, I really

appreciate it." I told Malik as we loaded the last of our first load.

"I just have to be done by at least eight tonight okay?" Malik said as he started up his car. He was living it up now. He had a new place and a Lexus SUV. I had been at *Juicy* longer than he had, and I still couldn't afford a new ride.

"What's happening after eight?" I asked.

"I'm meeting up with El."

"El? What kind of meeting?"

What kind of business meeting is held after eight o'clock at night?

"Nothing big trust me." He was short.

On the way over to the condo I decided to ask Malik about him and El's relationship. I know I should just mind my own business, but Mia is my girl, even though she was doing me wrong right now, I didn't want to see her hurt.

"Malik, don't get mad at what I'm about to ask you, but I have to ask." I prepped him and myself for what I was about to get into.

"What Andrea?"

"What's up with you and El? You two seem a lot closer than just friends."

"Really? Why do you say that? Because I'm gay, is that it. You think just because I'm a gay male that I can't have a friendship with a straight male, without trying to turn him out?" He was more upset then I had expected him to be. It felt like I hit a nerve.

"No Leak, I'm not saying that, I was just asking because.."

"Let me tell you something Andrea, I can't turn someone into something they weren't in the first place. I can't make someone gay that wasn't already that way." He snapped.

"What are you trying to say Malik?"

"I'm just saying, that El and I are just friends. Period."

"Okay, I didn't mean to offend you Malik, I was just asking okay?" I said hoping he wasn't too upset at me.

For the rest of the ride back to the apartment we talked and caught up on a lot of what was going on with each other. Mostly I was telling him about me and Jay, and he was listening.

"Here you go, take it for as long as you need it." I said to Malik as I handed him my camcorder.

He had asked to borrow it earlier that day. Even thought Malik said nothing was going on between him and El, I still felt something wasn't right. And it wasn't my gut telling me something more was going on, it was the flowers and candies addressed to Malik that I had seen in his trunk. I almost swallowed my gum when I read the card. It didn't have El's name on it anywhere, but it had his handwriting on it. This was too deep even for me.

Raheem

Looking at the all these buff ass cats made me realize I had to step my weight game up. I hadn't lifted weights since High School. Being surrounded by a bunch of football players can really fuck with a mans self esteem. I think I was the only one there that wasn't in the League, and I felt a little out of place. Needless to say I decided to just make the most of it. Jay had came over and promised me a good time, and I was on having one. There was so much alcohol there it looked like a damn liquor store. And these brothas were knocking those drinks back faster then the bartender could make them. I seen I was going to need a couple drinks in order to loosen up. Before I knew it I was toasted and feeling lovely.

I wish I would have waited until the dancers got there before I got drunk, cause when they came in I could hardly see them. Luckily I wasn't the only drunk one there. Those big ass men were like little boys when they saw the ladies walk in. They surrounded them so closely, I would be surprised if they even had room to dance. After about a gallon of water, about two bags of potato chips and four trips to the bathroom I had began to realize that those girls weren't there to dance at all. It seemed like everyone including Javonte knew that already. I tried my hardest to sober up so I could keep an eye on Javonte, but I was still too drunk. I just couldn't keep up with him. Finally after about an hour my vision became a little clearer, and I realized that Jay was no where to be found.

El

Rose pedals. His surprise for me was rose pedals spread all over the suite. Mine for him was, well it was Me. Me and a Rolex he had been eyeing for the past couple of months.

"I really needed that." I said as I put on my Sean John button down, and checked myself in the mirror. I was so fly, too fly for my own good.

"Yeah me too, I feel really good now." Malik said as he admired his new Rolex. "I'm sorry about ignoring you. I was just hurt." He finished.

"I know it's hard, but I promise its gonna all work out for the best in the end."

At least I hoped it did. I knew I had no intention of leaving my wife, let alone telling people about Malik and me, but now I know I can't tell him that. Last time he cut me off, and I can't have that happening again. I have to feed him pipe dreams in order for us to continue. I gotta do what I gotta do.

"You gonna shower or can I hop in." Malik asked.

"Go ahead." I answered. He knew I hated taking showers in these damn hotels, it made me feel cheap, and that was something I wasn't. Malik always took too damn long in the shower and it got on my nerves.

"Hurry up! You know the game has been over for more then twenty minutes now."

I yelled at the bathroom door. We were supposed to be that the sports bar watching the game, but the game was over. And I knew my wife would be waiting for me.

"Just meet me in the car. I need to get some fresh air." I said as I walked out of the suite and into what seemed like another world.

I had to get my mind right, because the way Mia has been on me, I just knew she was waiting for me to slip up. And that wasn't gonna happen. I was way too smart for that. We made it to my house just in time to watch the post game show on ESPN.

"How was the game you two?" Mia asked from the kitchen.

"It was good, we rushed all the way home to beat the traffic just so we wouldn't miss the post game show. All that rushing made me sweaty, I'm gonna go hop in the shower, I'll be right back."

Damn I'm good.

"Make yourself comfortable Malik." I heard my wife say as I rushed up stairs to wash this lust from my body.

While I showered, I began to feel bad about what I had did to Malik. Thinking back, I shouldn't have threatened him with losing his job. But I had needs that needed to be taken care of. When Malik and I first started out, he told me he just wanted to have a good time. As time went on, I saw him in a different light, and I know he felt the same way. But I'm a man, and real men don't deal with emotion, they deal with the facts. And the fact was, I was a married man with a family and no matter how much I felt for Malik, I would never leave them.

When I got out the shower, I felt refreshed, and of course fly as hell. As I toweled off my body and turned around I almost passed out. When I looked in the mirror prepared to admire myself, I saw something traced onto the mirror. As I rubbed the water out of my eyes I saw what had been written on the mirror. Through the steam that had formed onto my bathroom mirror I saw the words *I Quit,* traced onto the mirror. I nearly lost my mind when I read those words. I ran down stairs with the towel half way hanging onto my body. I checked in the living room where Malik was suppose to be, but he wasn't there. I ran into the kitchen and held myself up on the wall.

"Where is Malik, Mia?" I asked half way out of breath.

"What's wrong baby?" She asked.

I didn't have time for this.

"Where is he?" I screamed.

"He left, he said he had to go. Why what's wrong?" She asked again.

I couldn't answer her. The room was spinning. I had to calm down. I ran up stairs to my bedroom and sat on the edge of by bed with my head in my hands. What was I going to do? What was Malik going to do? I called his phone more than fifty times, but he just kept sending me to voice mail. I had to think real hard. Where would he go? Who would he call?

Andrea

"Andrea where is Malik?" El asked in a frantic tone.

"Why what's wrong?"

"Never mind all that, have you talked to him in the past thirty minutes?"

"No why what's going.."

He cut me off.

"Fuck!" I heard El scream before he hung up the phone.

If I wasn't sure something was going on between them before, I was sure now. I was in the middle of packing the last of my things, but I had to stop to find out what the hell was going on.

"Malik where are you?" I asked. I had called him about three times before but he didn't answer. Thankfully this time he finally picked up. I heard a lot of noise, so I knew wherever he was, he wasn't alone.

"I'm Downtown at the Gay 90's with my people, people who don't hide from who they really are." He said slurring half of his words. He was drunk.

"Malik, what are you talking about?"

I had no idea what answer was going to follow

my question, but if I had known, I wouldn't have asked.

"Do you really want to know?" Malik said.

He the then began to tell me about him and El's relationship. He told me about El's dreams, about their first kiss, and even how many times they had slept together. A lot of it was too much information for me, but I had to listen. He told me about how El and asked him to talk to Mia and to convince her he wasn't cheating. He told me how he got sick and tired of sneaking around, and that he had decided to be done with El. Then he went on to tell me about El blackmailing him into keeping the relationship going. I couldn't believe what I was hearing. Malik told me he hooked my camcorder up in the hotel room, and taped the two of them having sex.

"And you want to know what I did with the tape Andrea? When we went back to this precious home, I knew I would be left alone in the loving room, while he took his shower. When Mia finally went back into the kitchen, I hooked the camcorder up to that big screen TV, and I left him and his lovely wife a little note. All she has to do is push play, and his life will be over.." I hung up the phone. I couldn't stand to hear anymore. I had to call and catch Mia before she saw the tape. I couldn't let her find out about El like that. I had to warn her.

Mia

I knew when he ran upstairs he was going to call Andrea, and when I picked up the phone and heard her voice I knew my suspicions about the two of them were true.

"Why were you just talking to Andrea?" I asked El. He had looked like he was doped up. His eyes where bugged out and he couldn't stand still.

"Did Malik say anything to you Mia?" He yelled.

So Malik did know about Andrea and him, he was just covering up and probably got sick of it. That's why he left like that. And that's why El was running around here looking for Malik, he was scared he would tell me what was going on.

"You afraid he was gonna tell me about your cheating El!" I screamed at the top of my lungs.

I felt my eyes burning as the tears rolled down my face. I was fed up with being lied to and ran over. And I could see in his eyes that he was guilty.

"I'm sorry Mia." El said as he ran out the back door and left me with nothing but my own thoughts and my own reason on why he would do this. This cannot be happening, not to me. I have tried too hard to be a good wife and Mother to his son, and this is how he treats me? And with my best friend? Just then my thoughts were interrupted by the phone ringing.

"Mia you okay?" I heard Andrea ask. News sure spreads fast.

"Why wouldn't I be? I just found out my husband has been cheating on me Andrea!" I screaming so loud, I could feel myself becoming horse.

"I'm on my way." She said as she hung up the phone.

The nerve of her to try to come over and make things all better. Little did she know I had something for her ass. She had fucked with the wrong one.

Raheem

I shouldn't have drank as much as I did. This wasn't my type of party. I thought it was going to be a bunch of guys talking about sports and sex, but I was mistaken. There was nothing but a bunch of money hungry groupies here. Too many to even keep count. Mentally I could feel myself start to sober up, but once I tried to stand up I ended up falling right back down. I was looking as hard as I could, but I couldn't see Jay anywhere, and this condo wasn't so big that he could get lost in the crowd. But I did see something that gave me enough strength to get up and stumbling towards it.

"Nicki what the fuck are you doing here?" I couldn't believe that hoe was here.

"Working Raheem. Now unless you got more money then these ball players, I suggest you stand aside and wait your turn."

"My turn?" I had to be more drunk than I thought I was.

"I knew I seen you Nicki!" I said. It was all starting to make sense. She had gave that wack ass flyer to Jay's homeboy. She had planned this whole thing out. I had to find Jay. I knew once he knew that hoe was here, it was gonna be a wrap for her trifling ass.

El

I can't be mad at Malik for what he did. I left him no choice, He wasn't dumb, he knew I wasn't planning on leaving my family for him. I just don't understand why he left like that. He didn't tell Mia about us. He just left. Andrea hadn't heard from him, and I don't think she knows what's going on. She's too busy with her own life to be worried about who I'm sleeping with. But I swear that night at the party it felt like she knew something. She was acting really weird. But it seems like nobody beside Malik and I knew about what has been going on between us. As I drove back to my home I began to think more and more about what had happened. Malik had quit. That's it. He didn't tell Mia and he didn't tell Andrea. He just quit. What was the big damn deal, I was stressing over nothing.

I shouldn't have walked out like that. She didn't know anything. She was reacting on her assumptions, because there was no way that she knew anything. I just made it worst by leaving the way I did. I was on my way to my office to try to think things threw, and to look for Malik, but I had to take care of home first. I had to go back home and make things right, and if that meant coming out the closet and telling her about Malik, then that's what I would just have to do. There was a lot more at stake besides my family and friends finding out. Right now I didn't care about anything or anyone except Malik. It was time for me to come clean, even if I lose everything I have worked so hard to build. I was in love and I couldn't run from that truth anymore

Andrea

On my way to Mia's house I didn't know what to expect. I was praying so hard that she didn't see the tape, but by the way she was sounding I think she did. Mia has changed so much from back in the day. She used to be a straight hood chick. But once she got with El she slowly began to calm down. She stopped a lot of the bad shit she was doing, for El. She just really turned around. I'm just scared that once she finds out about El that she is gonna bug out and revert back to that hood chick she used to be.

"Open the door Mia!" I yelled as I pounded on the door. Then to my surprise it opened and Mia was right there waiting for me.

"Mia are you okay?" I asked her. I could see she had been crying. She didn't look good at all.

"How could you?" Mia said.

She was way too calm, and what was she talking about? I hope she didn't think I knew all along. She turned her back on me and walked into the living room. To my surprise I saw the video camera and the note still sitting on the T.V. It didn't look like she had even watched the tape, or even read the note for that matter. Now if she hadn't seen it, then what was she talking about?

"What? How could I what Mia?" I was

dumbfounded.

"My husband Andrea? You're my best friend!" She said through her tears.

I couldn't understand what else she was saying because she was crying and screaming. She was hysterical, and I was confused. When she turned and went into the kitchen I decided to go for the camcorder and the note before she seen it. I damn near tripped over the furniture trying to get to the note and the camcorder. Finally after trying not to make too much noise, I got it. Then with the note behind my back, I seen Mia coming towards me with a knife. What the hell was going on?

Mia

"What are you doing with that knife Mia?" Andrea yelled.

"I'm sick of people walking over me, I'm sick of being treated as if I don't have feelings. I'm sick of being nice, Andrea. You know why? Because people walk over you when you're nice." I said while stepping closer and closer to Andrea. "People don't take you seriously when you're nice. You best friend fucks your husband when you're nice, and I'm sick of it!" I screamed.

"Mia you have it all wrong, let me explain." Andrea pleaded.

"Explain what Andrea? You have always wanted everything I had since we were young. You were never my friend Andrea. I was just someone who you could boss around and tell what to do. You want to explain that, well explain it then!"

I screamed as loud as I could as I held the knife to her throat. Then I seen she was hiding something behind her back. She just can't stop hiding things from me.

"What are you trying to hide from me now Andrea?"

"I didn't want you to find out like this, Mia.

That's why I came over. You got it all wrong.."

I cut her off.

"Give me the note!"

With a knife to her throat she had no choice but to let me see it. I snatched it from her hands and read it aloud. *"This will explain everything. Push Play."* I saw the camcorder on the floor next to Andrea. I looked over at Andrea, and she looked scared and confused, but I didn't care about her, just like she didn't care about me. As I pushed play I thought back to the time when Andrea gave me the idea of taping El and me while we were having sex. She had probably taken her own advice and tried it out with my husband. I pushed play and sat down on my suede couch. The first person I saw was Malik. I was confused, what was he doing there? Why was he on the tape? Malik was setting up the camera in what looked to be a hotel room. This must have just happened because Malik was wearing the same clothes he had on tonight. I was waiting to see Andrea, waiting to see her lay a hand on my husband so I could cut her for each time she touched him. Then I saw my husband walk in front of the camera. Malik sat down on the edge of the bed, and El began to undress in front of him. My husband and Malik began to kiss.

"Oh my God!"

I couldn't believe my eyes. The whole time I

thought it was Andrea, but it was Malik!

"Tell me this is a joke Andrea, tell me this isn't happening!" I cried and fell into the arms of my friend.

"I'm sorry Mia, I just found out, that's why I came over I didn't want you to find out like this. I'm so sorry."

Andrea said as she hugged me and rocked me back and fourth. I was on an emotional roller coaster. I felt so bad for even thinking that Andrea could and would do something like this. I was so ashamed of how I acted and about pulling that knife on her, when all she was trying to do was help. I couldn't watch the video anymore. I didn't want to see what El had been doing behind my back. I couldn't handle it. I heard the sounds of them making love. I heard my husband scream out for another man. He was screaming out for the man I thought was his friend. They were speaking loving words to each other, kissed each other and held each other. Malik was getting treated the same way El used to treat me. He told Malik he loved him and looked at him, the same way he used to look at me. Day by day and month by month, I knew my husband was fading away, I was losing him. But I didn't think for one minute that he had lost his self in another man, the way I had lost myself in him. My husband was making love to another man and I had no idea.

Andrea

While I was comforting Mia, I looked up and seen El standing there. He had came through the back door. Luckily Mia's back was turned so she didn't see him. My shoulder was soaked with her tears and I was halfway deaf from her loud cries. I looked at El and I didn't recognize him. The man standing in the doorway, wasn't my homeboy from back in the day. He wasn't my best friend's husband or my God son's father. He was nothing to me, and as Mia screamed and cursed his name I could tell she felt the same way. He saw the tape playing, and he heard his wife's cries, but all he could do was turn away and leave. I sat there with my friend and held her. I didn't say any words, I just her cry. I let her scream, cuss and do whatever else she needed to do. Even though she thought I had been sleeping with El and even though she held a damn knife to my throat that didn't matter to me. All that mattered was that my friend was in pain. When I saw El look in on his wife, and turn his back I wanted to pick up that knife and stab him in the ass. I hated El for what he had did. It's not that fact that he was gay that makes him less of a man, not at all. What makes him less of a man was the fact that he knew all along that he had these feelings, and he didn't let his wife know. He went ahead and got married and brought a child into this world, knowing something wasn't right within himself. He was a punk for sneaking around behind her back. El wasn't a real man. He never really was.

"Don't trust them Drea! You can't trust nobody!" Mia cried.

"It's gonna be okay Mia. I'm here for you girl." I said as I continued to rock her back and fourth.

"What am I supposed to do now? I gave up everything. I gave up myself for him. I don't know what I'm suppose to do Drea? He is all I know, he was all I knew? Where do I go from here?" Her cries were hurting my soul.

After Mia fell asleep I finally left her house and I was emotionally drained. I couldn't think straight all I knew was that after that episode with Mia, I needed to see my baby. Who knows how many stop signs I ran through, not to mention all the red lights. I'm surprised I didn't get pulled over. When I pulled into Jay's condo parking lot and seen all those cars I had realized that he was having his party. With everything that had just happened, it slipped my mind. The way I was feeling I didn't care if he was having a party, I just needed to talk. And hopefully they had some liquor up there, because I needed a drank. Not a drink, but a drank! I just hope it wasn't too wild up there.

Raheem

After my run in with Nicki I decided I deserved at least two more drinks. I had ran into Jay in the bathroom and he looked like he was staying out of trouble. After he left, I had remembered my whole reason for searching for him. That was about an hour ago, and I haven't seen him since. I was sick of stalking his ass. I'm sure he was on his best behavior. Besides I was getting a lap dance from some girl, and it wasn't half bad. All of a sudden I heard a familiar sound. I heard Nicki's screams. Not like she was in pain, but her sex screams. Then it came to me. Whenever Jay would disappear, so would Nicki. If Jay was with that hoe, I was gonna beat his ass. I had to get up and I didn't care how many of his people I bumped into as I followed the screams. I finally got to the door after falling about six times. I had to take a couple deep breaths and try once again to sober up. I had to make sure I was okay, because I was about to kill this dude, assuming that it was him in the room with Nicki and not one of his boys. Just as I put my hand on the door knob I felt a soft hand under mine. When my eyes were finally focused, I realized it was Andrea.

"Damn Raheem, you're fucked up! Is Jay in here?" She asked and opened the door before I could even answer her.

And just like I thought that trifling nigga was in bed with that trifling hoe. Before I could say shit Andrea's ass grew wings and flew over and landed right on top of Nicki. Jay had the nerve to get up and start to get dressed, like he was about to go somewhere. Anger is a funny and sobering thing. All the water and chips couldn't have sobered me up as quickly as seeing his bitch ass try to leave out the room. I couldn't believe he didn't even try to get Andrea off of Nicki. Andrea was beating her ass, not that I was mad at that fact, but he as her man should at least try to calm her down. The only thing he cared about was getting out of that room.

"Where you going?" I said right before I punched his ass right in the mouth. When he fell on the ground I fell on top of his ass, and began to beat the shit out of him. I don't know what happened next but all I know is that for this fool be a football player, he fought like a bitch. I felt kinda bad for the brotha. Andrea and Nicki were on the other side of the room by now, and by the looks of things Andrea was handling her business. It had gotten so loud in the condo, nobody even knew what was going on. Until someone walked past the room seen all the drama. My fists were full of blood and Jay looked like he was knocked out. When I looked up I seen Nicki laying in the corner, fucked up. Hair was everywhere, and it wasn't Andrea's. It was Nicki's and she wasn't even wearing weave that night.

"Call the police! He's dead!" I heard someone yell.

"I'm not dead." Jay said. His punk ass was playing like he was knocked out so I would stop hitting him. What a bitch. I had to punch his ass once more for that move.

"Andrea lets go!" I said as I pulled her off of Nicki. I don't like the damn police, and they didn't like me.

"Wait Raheem. " She said as she walked over to Jay who was holding his face from that last hit.

"How could you do this to me Jay? You cheating on me is bad, but why with her?"

"Look Andrea. I'm sorry this had to happen. I mean I'm sorry I got caught. You have to understand that I'm in the League now, and this is what happens. Men cheat on their women, and you know why? Because he is paying all the bills and she is getting taken care of. Isn't what you said you wanted? Somebody to take care of you? Well here I am, you got your bills paid off, and you're about to move in with me, but don't expect me to not sleep around. I'm a man, what do you expect. I can have any chick I want, and I'll be damned if I'm gonna let you take that away from me. I love you Andrea. I really do. But this is my life now. You kept going on and on about how you wanted to be taken care of, about how you didn't want to work. You talked about all the material things you wanted and how many kids you wanted. Not once did you say anything about me loving you or being faithful. You are just as bad as these bitches in here. They at least work for their money, all you do is look cute on a nigga's arm. You told me what you wanted, and I gave it to you. Next time be more specific on what you want. You got what you asked for."

Jay said as stumbled off of the ground, and checked his self out in the mirror.

"Fuck you Jay!" Andrea said as she ran out of the room.

I ran after her to make sure she was okay. This was not supposed to happen. If the police weren't on their way I would have whooped his ass one more time, for that punk ass speech he had made. He was a punk. Even though she wasn't with me, I was happy she had someone that loved her the way I did. But after seeing and hearing what he had to say, I realized no one could love Andrea the way I love her.

Andrea didn't want to go to her apartment because she knew she would have to tell Trina about everything that went down at Jay's party, and she wasn't up for that. On the way back to my house we rode mostly in silence. I didn't know what to say to her, I just wished I could make it all better for her. She didn't deserve to be treated like that.

"Do you want anything to drink or eat?" I asked Andrea as she sat down on my couch.

"No I'm fine Raheem. We were like a mini Bonnie and Clyde huh?" She joked.

"You were more like Superwoman, the way you flew across the room."

We laughed. Andrea was laughing through her the tears she was trying so hard to hold back. After a while they couldn't be held back anymore. I held Andrea close to my heart, and I felt her pain. I didn't care about our past I just wanted her to be alright.

"El did what?" I said.

After Andrea was all cried out, she told me about Malik and El, and I almost got sick. That was my boy. He had a wife and a child, how could he be so selfish. I was angry at how he had treated Mia. How could you create someone's pain and then walk away when you're confronted about it? If I ever seen El again, I was gonna let him know exactly how I felt. It didn't bother me that he was gay, like I told him before, whatever makes you happy. What bothered me was the fact that he wanted so much from everyone around him, especially his wife, but he never gave half of what he expected from others. El was and is a selfish asshole and I have always known that. I just thought that as his friend it was my job to accept him for who he was. But now his actions are affecting more than just me, and it's not right. After we talked about El, we talked about Jay.

"I never thought he would do that to me, not in a million years Raheem."

"You can't build trust from words Andrea. It takes time. I know how love can make you blind, but sometimes you have to keep as much guard up as you can. Unfortunately I found that out by dealing with you."

"Well damn. You sure do know how to make a down chick, feel lower."

"I didn't mean it like that. I just mean you can love somebody with all your heart, and you can really feel deeply for that person. But if they aren't at that level, there is nothing you can do. Wait or move on, those are your two choices. And depending on the situation, most likely you need to move on."

"I hear you talking Raheem. It's just a bad situation for me."

"I'm sorry Andrea." I said. I didn't want to say too much more. Her heart was fragile and I defiantly didn't want to be the second man to tamper with it.

"It just hurts Raheem you know. I really thought I had something with Jay, and it had nothing to do with his career. I'm not gonna lie, at first I thought it would be dope to date a ball player. But after I got past the fact that he played ball, I really started to see him for who he was, not what he did. My feelings just got deeper and deeper from the things he would tell me. Even though he wasn't showing me as much love as he should have, I ignored his actions and held onto his words. It's funny, I'm always the main one preaching about actions speaking louder than words, and people only showing you the parts of themselves that they know you want to see. I just wish I would had taken my own advice. I was so pressed on having someone in my life, I took whatever he gave me, and turned it around into something that I wanted. He was just a man, but because he was my man I thought he couldn't do any wrong, and if he ever did do wrong, I was there with an excuse for him. "

"You must be so mad right about now." I asked her.

"You know what, I'm not mad. You know why? Because I know, I did what I had to do. I loved the best way I knew how, I was good to him in the best ways I knew how. I gave my all. So I can't be mad, because it's not my fault. I can't be mad at the choice he made. It's his life. But I am sad about the whole thing. I had planned to be with this man for the rest of my life and he played me like I was nothing to him. The thing is he came to me, he wanted to get married, he made that step. Why involve me in your bullshit, if you don't know what you want? The good thing is that time heals all wounds, and with the way be dogged me out, I don't think it's gonna take that long to get over."

She spoke with a strength I had never heard. Not like this.

"The other good thing is that I'm keeping this fat ass ring!" She said as she laughed through her tears.

She was hurt, and I was there to hold her. I couldn't take the pain away, but I at least could try to ease the pain. That whole night we talked about life, love and friendship. One thing we didn't talk about was us. The two of us had evolved into very different people. Andrea wasn't as hard hearted as she used to be, and I wasn't as passive as I used to be. I don't know what the future holds for me and Andrea, but all I know is we were becoming friends. Something we had never tried to be before. And if we never changed from that title that would be fine with me, just as long as she is in my life.

~A Sample of Aftertaste~

One Year Later

Andrea

The funny thing about time is, it can create something unnecessary and destroy something necessary without warning. Life is funny like that, but it's a joke I don't get. Maybe it's just me. Maybe I don't see what I'm suppose to see. They say people are in your life for a season and only God knows their reason, but that doesn't make things any easier. I thought I did everything that I was suppose to do in my life. I give without thought of receiving, I loved those who needed it, even when I'm wasn't getting treated right in return. I hate pity parties, and I'm not one to complain, but something's gotta give. I used to think that my friends would always be there no matter what. I was wrong. Which has been happening more often than usual. The thing about dealing with people from your past is you either grow together or grow apart. It's not because you aren't feeling them anymore, it's just that your paths become different. One path that has aligned perfectly was... Well that's a whole other story all together.